EROS

John L. Bowman

ISBN: 978-0-578-89466-9

CONTENTS

CHAPTER ONE

Eros

I am Eros, the god of love, and I am the one who gives you humans what you want most—love and sex. As Cupid I shot many of you with arrows—I shot an arrow into Media, which made her fall in love with Jason, into Venus's breasts, which caused her to become enraptured with men, and into Dionysus, making him mad for a girl. I caused Psyche to fall in love with the ugliest creature on Earth, and I am the one who smites maids' bosoms with unknown heat.

How you humans fall in love and have sex follows predictable patterns that I will explain to you with a little story that involves circumstances, personality types and levels of love. It is intense and will weave in and out of rapture, jealousy, betrayal, passion, adultery, intimacy, two-timing, sex, morality and unmet expectations. It is an insane kaleidoscope of emotions you mortals endure when you take the fall. It is also silly because love makes you act like fools and become engagingly mad. You follow its swift shadow that never runs smoothly but blindly over and over.

My story may confuse you because it includes many things you think have nothing to do with love, such as politics, civil strife, parents, feminism and class, but they do. There are many intangibles in your lives that influence how you think, feel and act, and my story will play them out in love.

Also, there are two things about me you should know. First, I am a mischievous troublesome matchmaking god who enjoys meddling in your affairs. I am inclined to kindness but am often edgy, irritable and opinionated. Second, I don't exist in reality. I am a myth and a figment of your imagination, so my portrait is really about you talking to yourselves about things you intuitively know but don't acknowledge—a kind of Platonic recollection.

The three protagonists in my portrait of love are real-life characters Ann, Henry and Betsy along with a host of secondary characters like Constance Worthington, Ryan Peterson, Tricia Roberts, Bill Huffy, Martha Wilson, John Brown, Tim Weller and Mark Finicus. They weave a predictable timeless plot of love that I must admit surprised me in the end.

Betsy Worthington was born in Headington, England just outside Oxford in an old manorial house surrounded by extensive manicured lawns and gardens. Her family was a wealthy old aristocratic line of landowner Worthingtons who had gained privileges, titles and lands for serving many English kings. One of her ancestors had been a British admiral that defeated the French in the naval Battle of Grand Fort in 1810 during the Napoleonic Wars, opening up much of the Indian Ocean sphere to British hegemony. With her sister Rachel and brother Phillip, Betsy was raised in a typical strict and controlling Elizabethan family.

Of all the girls of her class Betsy, turned out to be the most beautiful—a fair, soft-skinned, red-haired beauty. She had a perfect oval face, alluring eyes, elegantly coffered hair, warming dimpled smile, well-proportioned body and breasts and humble demeanor—she was the epitome of alluring femininity equaled only by Aphrodite. As a young woman she was widely admired and pursued by the boys, which embarrassed her and became a source of constant friction with her domineering mother Constance Worthington. They had the usual mother-daughter battles over clothes and friends and later over the boys she should date. He mother, recognizing her allure, angled for a royal wedding and arranged dates with aristocratic boys—and once the dauphin prince. Betsy was horrified and told her mother that these kinds of boys are artificial girl-like effeminates, which only angered her mother. Unlike her mother, Betsy rarely got angry—her disposition was naturally equanimous. Due in part to her natural character and aristocratic upbringing, she was always mild tempered and cheerful. Inside, however, Betsy felt trapped, repressed and frustrated. She had been raised to think manners were everything—how she acted was more important than what she thought or felt. She resented having been taught that politeness and civil intercourse are more important than who she is.

I don't mean to get ahead in my portrait, but here I must explain that my next protagonist Henry wrote a famous book in college on Kierkegaard's unauthentic and authentic and Heidegger's anonymous person, and he used many of the people he knew in his book as examples that I describe in this story. Betsy, for example, was Kierkegaard's fourth type of authentic person, who strove to show her true self in order to be authentic. As Kierkegaard's fourth type, Betsy, as a university woman, based her pride on something deeper, which created a distance between herself and others. She was concerned with her individuality and uniqueness, sought solitude and withdrew periodically to reflect and nurse ideas on what might be. She held herself somewhat apart from the world, but not completely, and prided herself on vaguely felt superiority. I will explain much of this later.

What is most interesting about Betsy and relevant to my portrait are her views on love. Due to her authentic nature, she was able to put the compliments and entreaties of boys in perspective. She was able to constrain her desires and appetites—her appetites were easily satisfied because she was not driven by desire. As a result she expected to solve her own life problems and demanded little from others. Betsy's character threw me off a bit because I discovered that one of her driving attractions to men was not justice, as many of us gods assume, but rather kindness. I had always thought they went hand in hand but was wrong. The thing that really surprised me was how Betsy got along with Henry.

Henry Phillips was born on the opposite side of the globe from Betsy in Portland, Oregon, into a lower middle class family whose most famous ancestor had been the president of a pipe fitters union. He grew up in a modest two-story wood frame house in a tidy working class neighborhood amongst blue collar laborers. He started working at odd jobs when he was twelve, enjoyed working and always did his best. His mother Eleanor was doting, and his father Bill was a piously religious, moral man who did his best to instill faith in Henry. Henry honored his father but resented his entreaties to believe, which resulted in a certain irreverence that grew into atheism; this became a major source of contention with his father.

Young Henry was rather tall and thin and was a little gangly with dark hair and a fair complexion, like Betsy's. Unlike Betsy, due to his rough and tumble upbringing, he was usually unconcerned with what others thought of him. As he matured his personality became peculiarly intriguing. He could be dangerous, brave, funny and cynical. As he became more educated another trait of his emerged: a remarkable intelligence and desire to learn. Over time he became a kind of precocious polymath citing obscure historic figures like Procopius's *Secret Histories* and Seneca's stoic philosophy from *Letters to Lucilius*.

Henry's character was like Betsy's: authentic in many ways. He graduated from a university, valued his individuality, had a tremendous sense of self-worth and easily controlled his desires. Unlike her, he preferred to mix with the world rather than remain distant. I noticed another symbiotic or mutually beneficial characteristic of Henry and Betsy's that also caught me off guard: Betsy valued kindness in others with little thought to their sense of justice, and Henry valued justice above all with little regard to kindness. I was curious how this might work out.

When Henry was in his late teens, fights with his father began to intensify. The issue was always faith and religion and both gradually became intolerant of the other's positions. These fights caused Henry to step back and evaluate his father from a different perspective. For the first time in his life, he noticed how unlike they were. Henry had none of his piousness, religiosity, timidity or usually soft, gentle ways. In contrast, his personality was outspoken, bold and more forceful. He also wondered why he did not look like his short, pudgy father. It was quite a mystery to Henry.

Ann Miller grew up with Henry and was his closest childhood playmate and friend. She lived in a dilapidated, unkempt house in a seedy part of Portland not far from Henry's. Her lineage was unknown, her relatives were scattered, and it was rumored her heritage was Romani. Ann and Henry spent a lot of time together playing in each other's homes. Ann seemed to come alive at Henry's under Eleanor's kindness and Bill's interesting conversations. At first oblivious, Henry enjoyed playing with Ann at her house, but as he got older he became more uncomfortable. Ann's mother Ellen was an unbalanced understanding but shrewish kind of woman, and her father Steve was withdrawn, brooding and usually drunk. Her parents would often break into violent fights, with a bruised Ellen blaming Steve for their poverty and Steve chastising Ellen for her infidelity. Henry noticed how Ann would go stony quiet when her father entered the room and only later learned that he often sexually abused her. It was a brutal dysfunctional family with little civility, no manners, lots of pain and some cruelty with no safe haven for Ann other than Henry.

Ann was a handsome woman with black hair and a swarthy complexion. She was average sized with an attractive female body. When she entered puberty things rapidly changed. Her attractive body became exaggerated with long legs, swaying hips, large breasts and soft, alluring voice. She became incredibly sexy, exuding female hormones that attracted the boys like bees to honey—boys found her sexually irresistible. This all confused Ann because on one hand she enjoyed flirting and male attention but on the other felt embarrassed with her sexuality. Ann confided often in Henry, who became a kind of anchor from which she could gauge truth in an increasingly confounding reality.

Due to her upbringing Ann was insecure, which caused her anxiety and a certain fear of life, people and circumstances. With this she became a Goldie Hahn-like, fey woman driven by desire and passion with impaired judgment. Because of her desire and appetites, she was naturally drawn to passion, love and sex. But she was confused because she came to think passion and sex were love, which alienated her from deeper and broader sources of happiness. The predictable result was that her appetite for love was never satiated, so she lived desiring more of what she could not achieve. Her distorted wishful thinking was a mere illusion that only brought failed expectations—for her it was always just more of the same. I never could quite understand Ann, who was happy with Henry but always driven to be happier.

Ann was Kierkegaard's second kind of unauthentic person who cannot see alternatives or alternate ways of life. She is the person who is defrauded by others, forgets herself and is depressed in a crowd because she cannot stand alone on her own. She lacks a sense of self, has little self-esteem and is thus not centered, which prevents her from drawing from within the necessary strength to face up to life. The consequences were devastating. Ann succumbed and was beaten by the world and the existential truth of her situation, so she embedded herself in others, chose slavery because it was safe but then lost the meaning of self. She died inside to live but remained physically in this world. All of this combined with her sexual appeal brought her too much possibility, mostly from the many boys pursuing her, which made her life a madhouse.

But when Ann was with Henry none of these unauthentic characteristics emerged. With him she was this wonderful young woman always smiling, happy and optimistically yearning for a better life and meaningful, loving relationship. Unbeknownst to Ann at the time, Henry was her savoir. He gave her stability, unconditioned friendship and protection from not only the testosterone-driven boys but also from herself. As you shall see with the loss of this critical friendship, Ann's life went on a long spiral downward.

Henry's life with Ann was to become increasingly emotionally tempestuous, much like the city of Portland's political environment. Henry, who had grown up in a stable Portland, began to notice cracks in its edifice. The liberal local newspaper began running stories deriding police brutality, local agitators like Lew Day criticized systemic racism and white supremacy and there were occasional violent demonstrations downtown or at City Hall. He learned from friends how Portland's university had changed to become a silent virulent source of anti-capitalist Marxist socialist dogma preaching class warfare and collectivism and feminism vilifying white men. Henry wondered why agitation had increased in his once peaceful city, unaware that he was witnessing the consequences of unrestrained democracy and people who cannot handle the freedom it brings. Many historians had warned people that they do not want to live in the interesting times Henry was entering.

CHAPTER TWO

Unauthentic Love

Ann and Henry's childhood friendship began to change in their teens. Ann's body became feminine, her voice softer and her deportment both teasing and coy, which along with her handsome face made her popular. Henry's body got bigger and masculine, his voice deepened and he started growing facial hair. Their conversations changed from light talk about people and experiences to their feelings and thoughts—mostly of each other. Spontaneously they awkwardly began touching each other often and enjoying the press of their bodies. They began hugging and playfully wrestling when alone. Their relationship became increasingly intimate with uninterrupted eye contact, tender holding and speaking in supplicating voices. I watched their relationship change from youthful friends to lovers with patience because I had seen it so many times before—sometimes it flourishes and sometimes not.

Love came to them abruptly one day when Ann called Henry and in a wavering voice said, "I need to see you, please meet me at our place." Henry ran to the high school, climbed the fire ladder to the crease in the parapet and quickly slipped into their hideout. It was their secret place they had spent much time together in their youth, mostly when Ann needed to escape her father. He found her shaking and crying in a curled up ball on the mattress and instinctively put his arms around her to comfort her. Ann gradually calmed down, and they started kissing and caressing.

I must stop my story here and tell you a little about the nature of attraction between the sexes and a little about character and the nature of love before I return to Henry and Ann's first sexual experience. Your love originates with what you call dimorphic attraction, which is two similar beings with distinct forms—the fact that males and females are the same but different in some ways is what initiates the attraction that often leads to love. For men, females' physical differences ignite their passion. Their fair faces, rounded bodies, breasts, large hips and smell are irresistible. Naturally the sexes' different genitals are a significant source of attraction. They are also attracted by some intangibles like sex appeal, humor and fecundity. One tangible attraction is you like those that like you, so attraction intensifies when a male meets a female who demonstrates she likes him with her look, touch and voice. Henry is a fair example of the short list of things that attract men to women: he is driven by hormones and the female face, body and breasts; the result is usually sex and sometimes love.

Women's attraction to men is somewhat similar but also quite different. They are attracted to males' physical differences such as larger size, strong face, height, muscled chest, firm buttocks, strength, deeper voice, often older age and masculine smell. They also are attracted to males with intangibles such as sex appeal, hormones, gentleness, societal position and ability to provide. Because females bear the young, they often are attracted to males who can financially support them. And again, like men, their attraction intensifies when a male demonstrates he likes her with look, touch and voice. Ann is an example of this female attraction to men. Like men, she is driven by hormones; she is first attracted by looks and sensuality but often considers friendship and character before sex. I must explain that it is more complicated than this. Unlike many women, Ann, as an unauthentic person, is only capable of achieving the second level of love, which I will explain shortly.

Curiously, few of you think about the nature of sex, which is simply the instinct to reproduce. Pleasure comes with sex only because it enhances your reproducibility, but you forget this reason and focus only on the pleasure, which makes your sex a kind of free for all for pleasure. As Eros I don't mind this so much, but it causes you a lot of problems, which I will explain later.

The nature of love is different than the nature of attraction. There are four levels, which, in ascending intensity, are infatuation, desire, love and true love. The first two levels are transient, they come and go, whereas the last two are enduring—they remain. Let me explain here that I am describing love between people. You do have other forms of attraction, such as to a thing or idea, that you call love, but it is not the same. Loving an unchanging object or eternal idea like justice is not the same as loving a living, breathing, fleshy, changing person. The former are static forms of love while the latter are dynamic, which I am describing in this story.

I will describe the first two levels of love here—infatuation and desire. Rich or poor, man or woman, smart or dim, you all experience fleeting infatuation, which is the lowest level of love. You call it puppy love, and it occurs when you become infatuated with another person. It is a one-sided feeling of awe, excitement and tenderness in which you think you are in love. Infatuation sex is like shaking hands—it only brings instant gratification and no lasting satisfaction. Ann is particularly prone to this kind of love.

The next level of love is desire. Desire love fulfills a deep yearning that is entirely physical. It originates with physical attraction that becomes ardor and eventually lust that brings great pleasure. Desire love is when the different genitals are a central attraction and you indulge in unremitting orgasmic sex. Its origins are physical because your brain releases dopamine, or the "pleasure chemical," that produces a feeling of bliss and norepinephrine, which acts like adrenaline and produces a racing heart and excitement. There are a lot of chemicals bouncing around your body when you are in desire love. Desire love is deeply felt but usually transient.

Ann and Henry's first sexual experience is an example of desire love. As friends they had long surpassed infatuation and are now engaged in gratification. As unauthentic people in desire love, Ann and Henry had different thoughts and feelings. Henry thinks little of love, being more focused on the pleasures of sex, whereas Ann, although eager, due in part to her past, was a bit insecure, fearful, uncertain and even a little scared. Because of this Ann had developed an unhealthy sense of self-loathing and was never able to move to the higher levels of love, which I will describe later.

Back in their hideout I thought now or never, so I hit Ann in the hip and Henry in the shoulder with arrows, and the result was immediate. Their necking became intense, clothes were quickly shed and, oblivious to the world, they started making love. Because I have seen the event so many times and find it rather messy, I left them alone for a while, and when I came back they had changed

from childhood friends to young lovers—they had fall-
en in deep desire love. They had satisfied their physical
instincts, and Ann was giddy with excitement, eager for
more. Henry felt differently; he looked pensive as if something was missing. I will explain the reason for this later
when he meets Betsy, so let's move on with my story.

Henry and Ann were an inseparable couple during
their later years at high school. They socialized with
their friends often, one of whom was Ann's friend Vicki
Brown. Vicki had married her high school boyfriend Josh,
and they appeared quite happily in love. One day Ann
approached Henry and said Vicki and Josh had tried to
have children but tests showed that Josh was impotent.
Ann said, "Vicki thinks you have good genes and asked
me to ask you if you would impregnate her." Henry was
stunned with the request and at a loss for words. He wanted to help and asked Ann what she thought. Ann said it
would help her friend a lot and thought he should do it.
Unthinking Henry said yes, and they arranged trysts with
Vicki and Henry, which resulted in a pregnancy within
a month. Vicki was happy to be pregnant and thanked
Henry profusely. Shortly afterward Josh and Vicki moved
to another state so they could be close to Josh's family. Ann
and Henry were sorry to see them go, but Henry was left
with some very pleasant memories.

I mentioned earlier that there are many intangibles
that affect your love lives, one of which is civil strife.
Portland's origins were decidedly conservative, even a little

provincial. In 1800s America, there was a mass migration of pioneers seeking better lives in the West. One pathway to the West was the Oregon Trail, which originated in Independence, Missouri, and snaked westward to Fort Hall in southeast Idaho where it split, with one leg going to California and another to Oregon. At that split, historical records describe roughly 250,000 crazy gold-seeking miners who took the southerly route to California's gold fields. The remaining conservative, religious, prudential farmers seeking roots took the northerly route to Oregon. These are the people who established Oregon and Portland's zeitgeist, which was decidedly peaceful and conservative.

Henry grew up in the calm and polite society of Portland. Downtown was clean, ordered and populated by businessmen in suites and women in attractive dresses and blouses. There was little crime and few vagrants. It was a prosperous city that emphasized law and order. Its roots were Republican emphasizing capitalism, individualism and freedom under law. Most Portland mayors were Republican along with most state governors like Iron Pants Martin, who opposed Democrat Franklin Roosevelt's New Deal and refused to meet with him when came to Oregon to dedicate Timberline Lodge. Certainly there was petty crime and some labor unrest, like when liberal Senator Wagner was shot at, but overall Portland was a microcosm of America's roots—people were Jeffersonian and not Marxist. This was the shining city Henry knew growing up, which later changed for the worse under the national Democratic progressive movement, which I will describe later. Later in my story I will describe how this intangible political development profoundly affected Henry's love life.

CHAPTER THREE

Oxford and Crew

Near the end of their high school years Henry noticed a gradual change in Ann. She seemed more restless, always horny and wanting more sex. At first Henry thought little of it until he began noticing her spending more time flirting with other boys. There were rumors that Ann had become promiscuous, which concerned Henry. Then one day out of the blue Ann told Henry she had accepted a date from Ryan Peterson to go to the annual Christmas dance. Henry was stunned and asked why, and Ann said it was because she wanted to get to know other boys. Henry was hurt and after some thought told Ann that if she does this, their relationship is over. He told her how much he values loyalty and that he felt awful pangs of jealousy. Ann just laughed and said it was no big deal and that he was making too much of it. Henry looked at her in disbelief, as if he was seeing a new person, someone he did not know. With that, Henry went silent.

I must pause here and tell you about Ryan Peterson because I see so many of his type. If you humans want a truly meaningful love and sexual life, this is the type of person to avoid. Ryan is an unauthentic level one, a flake, shallow and insecure. On the surface he is charming, funny and well dressed, but he is all show with no substance underneath. He is driven by desire and is an unbounded pleasure seeker who expects the world to accommodate his appetites; he is left perpetually anxious and mystified when it does not. Because he lacks self-esteem, he often puts others down in order to build himself up, which makes him a friend only as long as he benefits. Most of his ardent desire is aimed at women to satisfy his sexual appetite, so he relentlessly pursues women almost like a stalker. Because of his unauthentic personality Ryan and those like him dwell in the lowest levels of love, infatuation and desire and are usually divorced.

As an unauthentic person herself, Ann was naturally drawn to Ryan's charms, went to the dance with him and for a short time was dazzled. It was a slow dance when Henry entered the gym, and he stared at her in Ryan's arms for a long time, feeling intense heart pain and jealousy. When Ann saw Henry's eyes looking at her she instantly felt embarrassment, guilt and deep remorse. She suddenly realized she was in the wrong arms. She felt repulsed with Ryan's touch and was grief-stricken suddenly realizing she had lost the man she loved. With tears welling in her terrified eyes, she watched Henry turn and walk away. Wildly she pushed Ryan and ran after Henry, caught up and grabbed him, exclaiming through her red eyes that she loved him and had made a horrible mistake. She asked for forgiveness. Henry, stone-faced, told Ann, "We are different and done," and walked away. So, Henry's love for Ann died that night at the dance. I have seen it many times, but it still saddens me. The causes are so predictable—unmet expectations, desire, ignorance, betrayal, and taking someone for granted—the list is endless and the result is always the same deep hurt.

I must stop my story again here to explain a little about Ann and Henry's painful breakup. When Henry walked away, Ann crumpled to the ground sobbing and lamenting the loss of her childhood lover. She knew she deeply loved Henry and wondered why she pushed away the man she loved. Because Ann had been abused as a young girl, she had inherited internal contradictory struggles. She wants to trust but cannot, wants to love but fears being hurt and wants to be vulnerable in love but also to hurt before being hurt. Henry's take was different. He knew Ryan Peterson's shallow personality and, knowing Ann was attracted to him, he began seeing her through new eyes. He thought

Ann, like Ryan, is a woman he can't trust, so he stopped trusting her to protect his heart from her. He thought that pleasing his eye with a woman like Ann ought to be avoided because it only plagues his heart.

Henry decided he needed to get away and change his life. Even though he was only halfway through his senior year in high school he had applied to some colleges, including Oxford, but he had not received any responses. He went to his counselor, teachers and principal and said he wanted to graduate early. They all knew his story and wanted to help, so they gave him special assignments to complete and tests to take. Henry worked like a madman on a mission for the next four weeks, passed all examinations and graduated. He decided not to wait for Oxford's response, went to his mother and said goodbye, packed his meager belongings, went to the airport and took the first flight to London. As the plane ascended out of Portland, Henry looked back and felt relief that he was leaving.

It was not the same for Ann. Distressed, she saw Henry a few times in the school hallways and hoped to talk with him. After a while she no longer saw him, and it was only when she went to the school secretary and asked where he was that she learned he had graduated early and left for college. For the first time, she realized she had lost the one true love of her life. The finality of this sent Ann into an inconsolable sadness that lasted the rest of her life.

When he landed, Henry took a bus to Oxford's admissions office in Wellington Square and asked the receptionist if he could see the Deputy Chancellor of Admissions. She called his office and said, "A Mr. Henry Phillips is here. He says he applied as a student and would like to see you." To the receptionist's and Henry's surprise, Chancellor Wilson said, "Send him up." After sizing him up, the chancellor said, "We have your application, but I am sorry to tell you we were planning to turn you down. Our next year's class is full." Crestfallen, Henry said, "Thank you sir, but I intend to go to school here, and I will stay as long as it takes." Chancellor Wilson rocked back in his chair, looked long at Henry, looked again at his application and said, "I see you're from Oregon in the United States." Henry said, "Yes." After another pause, Chancellor Wilson said, "You have traveled her from the other side of the globe to join our institution. We like students who want to come here, let me see what I can do." With that, Henry gave him his cell number, said thank you and left.

Elated, Henry felt free of all obligations, which was both exhilarating and daunting. He had little money, no place to go and no friends, so he wandered about Oxford until he came to the Bear Inn Pub, which he later learned is the oldest pub in town and a historic watering hole for Oxford students. He went in, sat at the bar, ordered a pint of bitter and began pondering what to do next. He struck up a casual conversation with a well-dressed and man-nered young man next to him with a strong aristocratic accent, who turned out to be an Oxford student. Phillip Worthington asked what an American is doing in Oxford, and Henry described his meeting with Chancellor Wilson and his circumstances. It turned out Phillip was intensely interested in America, and their talk evolved into a deeply intelligent, widely ranging conversation about Theodore Roosevelt, race relations and the American *Constitution*. After hours of drinking and talking, Henry asked if he knew of any inexpensive places to stay, and Phillip said, "I have a large, comfortable apartment near the campus and would be delighted to have you stay with me." So, Henry crashed that night at Phillip's and awoke to a phone call from Chancellor Wilson, who told him he has been accepted and can start school in the fall. Henry thanked him and, unthinking, asked if he knew of any job openings. There was a pause while the chancellor chuckled, then he put Henry on hold for a bit and came back saying, "There is an opening for a tender at the rowing club. Go see John Reynolds, the rowing coach."

I must again interrupt my story here. I have to tell you, I have a special place in my heart for rowers. My mother Aphrodite in ancient Greece, and later Roman Venus, found competitive rowers' lean muscular bodies, strength, endurance, resoluteness and Stoic attitude irresistible. They remind her of Spartan men. They are irresistibly sexy when straining with the oars in unison, like a powerful invincible military unit gliding over the water. Like my ancestors, this is one of the reasons I find Henry such a compelling character. Back to my story.

The shell house was a beehive of activity when Henry arrived with many young men and one older, silver-haired, powerful looking man, who turned out to be John Reynolds the rowing coach. Henry later learned he had once been a famous rower. Henry explained his situation, and Coach Reynolds said you're hired and pointed to the hulls to scrub and equipment to store. Henry took up the job with alacrity. He enjoyed the company of the rowers and listened to their discussions about rowing and especially confusing ergs. One day he asked one rower what an erg was, and he explained that it's a machine that measures a rower's work by a split—"Why not try one?" he asked. From a distance Mr. Reynolds watched as Henry got on, rowed as hard as he could for a few minutes and saw the laughter when his 3.8 split was announced. It was a novice split, like running the one-hundred-yard dash in a minute.

That summer Henry watched the robust rowing teams on the Thames and became enamored with the sport. There was something romantically athletic about it, so while he tended boats he devoured books on rowing and spent hours on the erg to improve his performance. Mr. Reynolds noticed that Henry would spend most of his free time groaning and sweating on the machine and began thinking that while he may be somewhat scrawny, he has the height, long arms and room for muscle mass, which are hallmarks of top rowers.

It had been a great summer for Henry working at rowing and spending time at the Bear Inn Pub with Phillip drinking bitter and discussing life, girls, philosophy and rowing. They were compatible characters, self-assured and interested in the same things. Phillip did have an aristocratic bearing, but he was a realistic humanist who valued relations over position. They liked each other and their friendship became more intimate as time passed, eventually maturing into a lifelong camaraderie. One night at the Bear, inebriated Phillip enthusiastically blurted out that Henry must meet his sister because they are so much alike. Henry shrugged and said sure.

It was becoming cooler, the leaves were turning colors and fall was in the air, which made the Oxford campus a timeless, magical place. Radcliffe Square looked like a white medieval fortress separated from the town with a thirty-foot wall, cast iron gate and pristine lawn that no one walks on. It is a place with thousands of famous books and more authors, like Shakespeare, Proust and C. S. Lewis, per square foot than any other place in the world. Oxford has thirty colleges, like mysterious All Souls that had been founded in the 1400s, and Oriel College or the King's College that had accepted Henry. Socially it was very different with formal hall and fancy dinners once a week when everyone dressed to the nines in uniforms and academic garb.

Henry was entering a new world of higher education surrounded by a variety of very smart people. His first courses, grounded in medieval European Oxford, focused on a liberal arts education and the seven liberal arts of grammar, logic, rhetoric, arithmetic, geometry, music and astronomy embodied in the classical trivium and quadrivium. He took the required Latin courses because all students were expected to speak it fluently and eventually the classics of history, philosophy and literature. It was only later that he was immersed in the modern sciences of physics, chemistry and biology. He began studying long hours, attending challenging classes, writing papers, meeting with his professors and sitting for exams. It was a period of tremendous intellectual growth for Henry.

One class that particularly interested him was on the history of philosophy in which he learned about Soren Kierkegaard's five kinds of authentic and unauthentic people and Martin Heidegger's anonymous ones. He was struck with their resemblance to the love lives of people he had known like Ann, Ryan and himself. It was this revelation that propelled Henry to unintended fame.

Rowing, which is called crew in America, is an old sport that originated in ancient Egypt. It was introduced to England at Oxford in the eighteenth century and quickly became popular. Early races included the head race of five kilometers with coxless pairs of three or eight rowers and a coxswain who steers the boat and keeps the crew synchronized and motivated to pull harder. The technique of rowing is timeless, in simple terms it is the drive, recovery, rest and then drive, technically it is the catch (when ready for the drive), the drive (when you press your legs, swing back to vertical and arm pull), recovery (when you move your seat position forward to the catch position) and then drive again. It is a sport that utilizes every major muscle in the body including arms, legs, abdomen and even tips of fingers—every muscle counts. It is a demanding sport; only one sweep of the oar and a small tilt of the head can offset the boat and cause it to dip to one side.

Henry decided he wanted to try for the rowing team, so he pursued his new passion for rowing, spending all his free time in regular and intense workout sessions on the erg. Coach Reynolds watched Henry with increasing interest because he liked determined and tenacious athletes. He also saw that Henry was getting bigger, stronger and better, so he took him under his wing and started coaching him.

He first told Henry the key to success is your split on the erg. He explained that the erg stands for ergometer, which is the device that measures work by counting how much the belt in the equipment is moving. Once you start pedaling it calculates the force you apply on the pedals (or rows) and the distance you pedal. It measures the work done by multiplying the force and the distance. It mimics rowing, but initially Henry was confused due to the many numbers on the display. The coach explained there were only four that really counted. They were the time measuring how long he had been rowing, the distance in meters he had covered rowing, the number of strokes per minute he had rowed (he should try to get to thirty, which is a high rate of strokes) and the large, all-important split number that measured the time it took him to row five hundred meters. Coach Reynolds told him this was important because it told him how fast he was going. Henry soaked it all in and doubled his efforts.

For the average person a 2.0 erg is pretty good, and for an elite rower it is possible to get 1.3. Later that year at the opening of rowing season, Henry asked Coach Reynolds if he could join the rowing team. You can only imagine the coach's reluctance, remembering Henry's 3.8 erg. However, knowing he had been trying to improve, the coach said, "Get on that erg and give me your best split." In front of all the crews Henry got on, took a deep breath and rowed as hard as he could. When he was done, unusually quiet Coach Reynolds read out: "1.2 split, thirty-three strokes per minute. Welcome to the team." Henry had just achieved the best split and stroke rate the now speechless coach had ever seen.

So, Henry had made the rowing team. Rowing had changed his physique; rather than tall and lanky he was now tall and powerfully filled out with large, lean muscles. He had also developed a lifelong love of rowing, which brings up a question about the nature of love. Earlier I said loving a thing, like a painting, play, idea or rowing, is not the same as loving a person because loving an object is not the same as loving a living, breathing, fleshy, changing human. But it is more complicated than this. Unlike humans, things don't talk, but actors talk in plays. Unlike humans, some things are unchanging, but paintings change depending on the light or angle of viewing. Unlike humans, things have no feelings, but many non-human animals do. Indeed, people say they love their pets which, like humans, have feelings, needs and sex. But I still claim love between humans is a different kind of love.

The problem is people use the word love as a catch-all for so many levels of tender feelings and intensities. The word has become so broad, it has become almost meaningless. People say they love plants, history, their hair, their mom and rowing and then use the same word to describe human love. Even within human relations, people say they love their friends and children like they say they love a movie. People use the same word for many different complicated types of relations, which has adulterated the word.

I am Eros, god of love and sex, and I will tell you that true love can only be achieved between the incredibly intimate and intense relation between two sentient humans of the opposite sex—a man and a woman. It is different, special and the highest kind of love. I say this for three reasons. First, unlike a painting, play, sport or an animal, it is the only love in which you can procreate and reproduce yourself. Spartan men who were homosexual claimed they loved each other, but they had to visit women to reproduce. You could disagree with me and say males can procreate with a female friend he "loves," and my response is that this is the only relationship where one kind of love can become true love. The second reason is, as I described earlier, passionate attraction and love comes in part from dimorphism, or another who is like you but different. Paintings, plays, sports and members of the same sex are not dimorphic. Finally, love between humans of the opposite sex deals with potential and purpose, which are to procreate children and create biologic families. Sex, for example, is done for a purpose and not just pleasure. Heterosexual human love brings a new ingredient of meaning to love that is missing in other kinds of love. However, there are still grades or levels of love between men and women. I have described two of them earlier, infatuation and desire, and will describe the next two, love and true love, later.

So, you don't believe me, just like all the others before I hit them with my arrows. Let me give you an example of why this is true when Henry meets an authentic woman and finds authentic love.

Chapter Four

Prelude to Authentic Love

Henry worked hard at learning rowing. He was put in many shells with different rowers and had to learn the skill and how to follow Chris Hooch the coxswain's instructions and keep in synchronization with all other rowers. He spent hours on the Thames in all kinds of weather rowing and gradually getting better. He learned how to avoid missing strokes and getting crabbed. It was physically taxing, and he was exhausted at the end of the day. The elite boat was the varsity eight-man skull, and one day coach Reynolds decided to try Henry out at the number two position just behind the team's star rower,

Jim Heart. Henry learned to mirror Heart's rowing technique and pace so well he got the coach's attention.

Authentic love began at a British Universities and Colleges Sport Championships in early November. It was a historic regatta between the Oxford, Cambridge, Durham, Glasgow and Edinburgh Universities rowing teams with an unusually large crowd of partisan and vocal fans. Coach Reynolds had taken a chance and put Henry on the eight-man Oxford rowing skull in the two-thousand-meter race. He was not sure what to expect and became concerned when the team started slowly at around thirty strokes per minute, well behind the others. It was like they were out of sync and floundering in spite of the coxswain's blandishments.

It looked like they did not have a chance, when about halfway through the race Chris Hooch yelled, "Thirty-two!" and Jim Heart went into a strong rhythmic rowing pace that everyone, including Henry, mimicked perfectly. The rowers had found the mystical swing where the boat flies without interruption. The skull lurched forward like a slingshot to Coach Reynold's and the Oxford fans' astonishment. They quickly gained on the lead skulls and finished first with an amazing time of 5 minutes and 30 seconds. Everyone was wildly jubilant, including Phillip and his sister Betsy, who were watching from the stands.

Phillip had pointed Henry out to Betsy, who had caught her eye. Like my mother Aphrodite, she found him a kind of heroic lean and strong Spartan warrior defeating his enemies. When they docked Phillip took his sister to meet Henry and was unsure what to think when the two stood silently looking at each other for a long time. Henry was stunned with her captivating beauty, and Betsy was mesmerized by his handsome face and powerful sweaty body. I have seen this prelude to love so many times, and it never ceases to amaze me. As they stared at each other, all of the forms of attraction between the sexes I mentioned earlier kicked in—dimorphism, physical appearance and eyes that say, "I like you too." Unbeknownst to them, they had quickly traversed the first level of love, infatuation, which many mistake for love at first sight, and were on the cusp of tier two love, or desire. They were two humans who were beginning the textbook ascent through the four levels of love. I was curious how far they would go.

When Henry started winter term he took a philosophy class from Don Steve Harper and studied Soren Kierkegaard and Martin Heidegger, who I mentioned earlier. He was struck by their descriptions of unauthentic, authentic and anonymous kinds of people, which poignantly described people he knew, like his father and in particular why he was not like him. He pondered the question why he loved his father, who was not an authentic person or one who lives by convention and never achieves a sense of true self. Henry's ideas gradually segued into how each type of person, both male and female, the philosophers were describing experiences love, so he decided to write a book titled *Unauthentic, Authentic and*

Anonymous Character Types and Love under a pseudonym, because he did not want to hurt his father's feelings.

I will describe his book throughout this story, beginning with how Kierkegaard's lowest two kinds of unauthentic people experience love. The lowest unauthentic person blocks off perceptions of reality, which results in character defenses and armor, does not see reality on its terms, is one dimensional and is totally immersed in the fictional games being played out in society. Because those people are ignorant of reality and others are not other-regarding and selfish, which makes their love shallow, their love is naturally infatuation or desire. They do not know what it means to think for themselves and therefore shrink back due to audacity and exposure, so they are not introspective, which prevents them from discerning the levels of love and what is meaningful in life. They are unable to transcend their social conditioning, avoid developing their own uniqueness, live with automatic styles and uncritical thoughts, are confined to culture and slaves to it, are lulled by the daily routines of society and are content with its satisfactions; thus, they are tranquilized into the trivial. They live by convention, like the masculine stoic archetype persona that inhibits intimacy and love. Finally, they do not belong to themselves and are not their own person, which means they don't love themselves and thus cannot love another. Ann's suitor Ryan Peterson was an example of this shallow loveless type.

Ann Miller is an example of Henry's second unauthentic type. She has too much possibility, and the result is her life is a madhouse. Her many suitors confuse her, she wonders who to love, she confuses infatuation and desire with love and she is indecisive and thus noncommittal in relationships. She succumbs to and is beaten by the world and the existential truth of her situation, doesn't understand reality, finds affections confusing and thus cannot discern what constitutes true love. She is often bogged down by daily duties and the demand of others, which narrows her horizon. Because she lacks imagination she has little insight and thus cannot see alternative futures, cannot imagine any choices or alternate ways of life and cannot release herself from her network of suffocating obligations. She never realizes the need to escape them and selfishly love another in order to achieve love. She is often defrauded by others, forgets herself and is usually depressed in a crowd because she cannot stand alone on her own center and cannot draw from within herself the necessary strength to face up to live. So she embeds herself in others, chooses slavery because it is safe but then loses the meaning of "I." She does not know you must first love yourself before you can love another, which leads to a barren, loveless life. Ann has died to live but must remain physically in this world; she is a living dead person existing as a hopeful shell seeking to be saved and never experiencing true love.

These two unauthentic types are depressing. They need to know true happiness and love come from being self-sufficient, having strength, being worthy of respect and just being joyful—knowing this, their love lives would unfold. If they could only control their desires knowing nature is easily satisfied and appreciate what they have they could experience the higher forms of love. But, alas, they never learn and spend their sordid lives trapped by convention, unable to be free individuals capable of love. Indeed, Henry concluded his book with the thought that an individual is what he thinks, which means he should use his mental powers to escape living in the world of others' opinions and be free to love.

Henry often talked about his book with Phillip, who found it quite interesting, at the Bear. When it was done, Phillip asked Henry if he could show it to an editor he knew at Oxford University Press, and Henry said sure. The editor loved it and asked Henry for approval to print it, and Henry signed a contract specifying a pseudonym author. They printed it and sent a copy to a literary agent in New York, who submitted it to Ingram Publishers. They loved it. They signed a contract with Oxford University Press, printed twenty-five thousand copies and began a publicity campaign. Because American society was experiencing chaotic violence, people were looking for some escape, which Henry's book offered; to everyone's surprise, book sales exploded, and it hit the *New York Times* Best Seller list. It was a runaway success.

Henry was mystified and frankly embarrassed so he, along with the few who knew the true author, kept the secret. This mystery caused considerable interest in the reading public. Professor Don Steve Harper was the only one who was not privy to the secret but knew the author was Henry; he was amused and decided to do nothing about it.

CHAPTER FIVE

Authentic Love

I knew Betsy and Henry would fall in love, but I was not sure how deep it would become. As time passed it became clear they were destined for its higher forms. They had quickly passed through the lower levels of love, infatuation and desire, which are the levels prostitutes and sex workers exploit and which many humans never move beyond. Knowing what I know now, I am going to describe their blossoming romance in detail, because it is a superb example of achieving true love.

First of all they both were ready for love—they were searching for it. Disappointed Betsy had dated the many effeminate, boring boys her mother wanted her to, and

Henry was ready for a genuine relationship after the painful loss of Ann. At first Betsy was startled at Henry's bold, swashbuckling, daring and strong personality, but she was also awed with his strength and athletic ability. There was something indescribably irresistible about him. Henry was immediately attracted to Betsy but wary of beautiful women. However, her calm, measured and confident bearing quickly assuaged his concern along with her comforting face and smile. Fate had set them up for love with a little help from a couple of my arrows.

There was a lot going on in their early phase of love, and the first was physical. Betsy was attracted to Henry's six-foot height, lean muscles, full hair and handsome face. Henry liked Betsy's sexually alluring figure, comely face, red hair and soft skin. As they learned more of each other, Betsy was taken with Henry's integrity, humor and apparent kindness, while Henry liked her loyalty, humor and confident demeanor. Naturally there were many intangibles attracting them including passion, smell, voice and sex appeal that play in attraction between the sexes. In sizing up each other's characteristics, each had an unconscious checklist before sex that always varies with you humans. In descending importance, Henry's was rather straightforward: looks, sex appeal, character and then sex. It was very similar to Ann's checklist; looks, passion, sometimes character and then sex. But Betsy's checklist was more comprehensive, longer and discriminating; first was character (she was looking for a good husband and father provider), then kindness (which she initially mistook as Henry's courtesy), humor, friendship, integrity, position in society, looks, sensuality, and if all the boxes get checked, lastly sex. Ann, due to her background, had low expectations, whereas Betsy's were high. This was an important step in the long road to true love because if expectations are not met, love usually dies. To complicate matters, sometimes expectations are fraudulently met, which, when discovered, diminishes love. I thought this might be the case because Betsy had misinterpreted Henry's courtesy and sense of justice as kindness—I thought to myself, only time would tell.

One significant last aspect of Henry and Betsy's love-puzzle-dance was their take on desire. Both felt tremendous desire for the other, but as authentic character fours, both were initially cool and self-controlled because they knew the consequences of bad desires—just wanting more of the same, like sensual pleasure, does not bring enduring happiness. However, being authentic they also knew, like epicures, that some desires are good, like the desire to love another or to live a meaningful life. Knowing this they both took a chance, a leap of love, willing to see if their desire would lead them to true happiness. I was impressed that they had made this difficult hurdle.

They spent a lot of happy time together hiking the backcountry around Oxford, rowing on the Thames and having intimate dinners at the restaurants and pubs around town. With Betsy's connections, they led a gay social life going to many parties, balls, dances and horse shows, always having fun together, touching and laughing as young people do when they are in love. Henry also spent time at Betsy's home getting to know her father and mother, Harold and Constance, her sister Rachel and of course Phillip, who was the architect of their relationship. Harold Worthington liked Henry and treated him like a son, but Constance, who was cordial, remained strangely distant.

Their love solidified over a few days in late October. Betsy had watched Henry row in the final Oxford-Cambridge regatta, which Oxford won thanks in part to the athletic ability of Henry. The crowd roared with applause, and Betsy was bursting with admiration and love for Henry, watching his boat glide past the finish line. After the race they took a long walk together along the Thames; it was an unusually warm autumn evening when they paused, looked at each other and kissed. It was the most passionate kiss either had ever experienced. It was a long, intimate, electric and tender kiss that sent shivers through their bodies. At that point they surrendered to each other.

I found the next phase of their evolving love so typical of you humans, which involves a kind of love—gamesmanship. That weekend Henry went to Betsy's father's sixtieth birthday celebration at her house. It was a grand affair with many friends, relatives and oddly eligible young men, who Henry later learned Constance had invited. When he got there Betsy was warm and smiling but down deep concerned she had let herself be taken too quickly. She decided to play coy and began flirting with the young men with a keen eye on Henry, who chuckling immediately began flirting with her sister Rachael. Jealously she began ignoring Henry and flirting more with the boys, who were in hot pursuit. Dismayed, Henry decided to leave, went to her parents and thanked them for inviting him, slipped out the back door and drove home. What silly games.

Amongst a throng of admiring boys Betsy surveyed the party to find Henry, and when she could not, she became concerned. She excused herself, wandered around trying to find him and eventually asked her parents if they had seen him, and they said he had left. Betsy felt a sudden feeling of remorse that overwhelmed her because she knew the story of how Ann had betrayed Henry and lost his love and was terrified she would also. She ran to her car, raced to Henry's apartment, banged on the door, and when Henry opened it threw herself into his arms and said "I love you." With these three simple words, their gamesmanship stopped and their deep love for one another began. Henry's heart melted, he said, "I love you too," and they went into the bedroom to have sex. As authentic four humans, they were ready for it, but again, I have seen this messy part of the love process too many times. I decided to leave.

So, they made the third level of love like two parts of a space station that had been engineered to fit perfectly and seamlessly by Zeus, like stars aligning and dots connecting. They became two authentic fours coming together—I was delighted and curious to know what would happen next.

I described the first two levels of love earlier and will now describe the next or third level along with how some unauthentic and authentic characters experience it using Henry's book *Unauthentic, Authentic and Anonymous Character Types and Love*. This is the kind of love you humans commonly think it is. It is romantic relationships along with tender and passionate affection for another person. It is a strong and positive emotional and mental state involving affairs of the heart such as friendship, kindness, devotion, regards, good wishes, admiration and respect for the beloved. These love partners take great pains not to hurt, abuse or humiliate the other. Deep and meaningful sex is usually a component of this level of love, but not always; this is the same love parents experience for and from their children. It is not a love that can be manufactured; it occurs spontaneously and naturally from the inside, apart from external influence. This the level of love Henry feels for his parents Bill and Eleanor and how now Betsy and Henry feel about each other. I must tell you, after eons of watching you humans experience this level of love—it truly is a gift.

Before I move on to describe how Henry's next character types experience love, I want to explain to you that your level of love depends on you. It derives from many influences like your attitudes, beliefs, experiences, up-bringing and circumstances. The lowest level of love, for example, is selfish infatuation with another. The next level, or desire love, is when you love another for what they can do for you, which is usually sexual gratification. The next level occurs when you love yourself first—you must love yourself before you can love another. This is where Henry and Betsy are now, but they are slowly moving to the next level, or true love. True love is when you love another for who they are. When you are able to transcend your self—when your selfish nature fades and you learn to value what another needs. There is one higher level that surprised me, which I will explain later.

In his book *Unauthentic, Authentic and Anonymous Character Types and Love*, Henry described two typical character types, unauthentic three and authentic four, and how they experience love. His unauthentic three is the average person who lives a conventional life. They are intimidated by experience and life and afraid to engage or commit; they are just trying to get through life safely to the grave. They are a kind of mildly neurotic person who has given up on life. These are those who are consumed with propriety and correctness, live safely within the probabilities of a given set of social rules, avoid the extremes, follow a middle course and tranquilize themselves with the trivial. Kierkegaard called them Philistines. It should come as no surprise then that these people are timid and intimidated by potential lovers, fear showing or giving themselves to another, find it hard to make commitments and are generally numbed to the experience of loving. Henry's father's need for religious faith is an example of this type.

The second type Henry described is the authentic four character, who is a stable, centered and confident type of person best able to deal with reality's challenges. This type has contempt for convention, is somewhat detached, is educated and not religious, is bold, is a seeker who wants something better, is introspective, has self-esteem, looks for truth and is industrious and ambitious and generally revolts against existence. In addition to resisting convention in order to be authentic, this type of person is a paradigmatic character who endeavors to live life to be happy, has contempt for immediacy, tries to cultivate interiority, bases their pride on something deeper and creates distance between themselves and the average person. Henry's authentic four character is the formula for an authentic person because it resists daily dying and prefers to live life on its own terms.

With these characteristics, authentic four people are able to achieve higher forms of love. They fall in love with and marry those who they want and not who others want, they know who they are compatible with, they seek true love, when they find the one they love they commit themselves, they think they are worthy of love (which makes them loveable) and they have attractive traits like provider or nurturer that the opposite sex looks for in a lover.

This is the level of character authenticity Henry and Betsy achieved—and with it, level-three love. But there are some concomitant characteristics at this level that militate against love. These character types tend to be introverts, are often more concerned with their individuality and uniqueness, enjoy solitude and sometimes withdraw to reflect and nurse ideas on what might be. They hold themselves somewhat apart from the world but not completely and pride themselves in vaguely felt superiority. But as authentic fours, Henry and Betsy know these impediments to love, so they naturally keep their goals in perspective, consciously minimalize their weaknesses, focus on the good in the other, are more accommodating and just love the other for who they are. With this Betsy and Henry had achieved the sweet spot of love and happiness that you humans so ardently desire.

However, their burgeoning love was shattered one autumn day Henry's senior year after a regatta. They were walking alone along the Thames when Henry stopped, dropped to one knee, showed Betsy a ring and asked startled Betsy to marry him. To Henry's astonishment Betsy hesitated; he was flabbergasted and speechless. Crying Betsy hugged Henry and then ran away. Henry did not know what to think so he drove straight to her house and banged on the door. Constance Worthington opened it; Henry said he wanted to see Betsy, and Constance said no just as Betsy appeared. Henry brushed past Constance, took Betsy's hand, looked her in the eye and in earnest said, "Betsy, I love you—what is the problem?" Now red eyed and crying, Betsy said, "Henry, I love you too, but my mother forbids our marriage." Just then Constance broke in and said in a surprisingly concerned tone that Henry was a good man but not socially prominent enough to marry her daughter. With that Henry looked at Betsy and said, "Who you marry is up to you and not your mother," to which now sobbing Betsy said, "I cannot defy my mother," and ran upstairs. Heartbroken, Henry took a long and contemptuous look at Constance Worthington and then left their house forever.

It was a sad scene so common in love that I suspect many of you are wondering what has this to do with true love. All I can tell you is that true love never runs smoothly—it always faces obstacles. So, bear with me and let me continue my story, so you can see how things work out.

CHAPTER SIX

The Tragedy of Authentic Love

After the breakup with Betsy and confrontation with her mother, Henry felt hurt and lost. Phillip was not much help because he knew his mother and sister and acknowledged there was little he could do. After a listless, unhappy month, Henry decided he needed to get on with his life so, like back in high school, he applied himself to his studies and finished his exams. In early June he graduated with a master's degree in finance and a minor in philosophy, said goodbye to everyone including Phillip, Coach Reynolds, some professors and teammates, and left. He had seen Betsy once after the breakup with a boy at the Bear Inn Pub, which caused him sorrow, but he just left as Betsy watched in obvious dismay.

Henry had planned to go into the financial business, which had an epicenter in New York, so that is where he went. It was a lonely time for him. He got a small, inexpensive apartment, applied to numerous large securities firms, was hired by Silicon Equities and started working. His life quickly became a monotonous cycle of sleep, eat, work, eat, sleep. He became a kind of automaton, mindlessly buying and selling securities bereft of any human feelings like friendship and love. Knowing you humans, he could have lived this way the rest of his life if it had not been for two events. The first was a call from his mother Eleanor telling him his father Bill had died. He flew home to Portland, comforted his mother, helped arrange a small funeral and thought a lot about his dad, who had loved him and now gone forever.

The second event was Tricia Roberts. Back in New York after the funeral, Henry quickly fell into the same monotonous work routine, so one night he decided to go out and ended up at the notorious pickup bar, the 40/40 Club, in Manhattan, where he met this athletic-looking attractive blonde who took an immediate liking to him. He was naturally wary because of his experiences with women but enjoyed her robust personality and sensual nature.

It was an odd relationship that flourished between the two due to their different natures. Henry was his usual centered, charismatic, outgoing self, whereas Tricia was a compilation of multiple personalities. At first Henry thought she was normal, but as he got to know her she became more like someone on steroids. She could be edgy, nervous and energetic, unable to relax. He did not mind this so much until she occasionally became a hard-driving, bossy, assertive and intimidating personality that he did not like, but he understood these were the characteristics that had enabled Tricia to become the successful and rich attorney she was. As time passed, he noticed that one of her defining characteristics was, much like Ann, a driving desire for more of everything, but times ten. She was never satisfied and was always talking about getting more clients, more money, more sex and a better apartment. She was incapable of being satisfied—even sex with her was like combat. He also observed that her rare periods of peace were because she was strung out from taking drugs. He watched her smoking pot and sometimes snorting heroin in order to escape herself. He watched as gangs of demons would start boozing in her brain. Normally Henry would have just said goodbye to such a strange woman, but there was another side of her that intrigued him. Tricia could be extremely warm, soft and loving. She would occasionally display a deep sincere yearning to love and be loved that he found compelling. One day while looking at her, pondering her chaotic mind and eagerness for love, Henry suddenly realized Tricia was the rare authentic character type five he had written about in his book. It all became clear to him that love for her type was destined to be tragic—she was born with the capacity for love but not for love itself.

In *Unauthentic, Authentic and Anonymous Character Types and Love*, Henry had written that authentic five character types, in their effort to become God, are assertive, self-created and endeavor to master their fate. They plunge into life with a restless spirit, which often manifests itself in wonton sensuality and debauchery. Sometimes they become demonic in their revolt against existence, all of which conspire to thwart love. Their aggressive, edgy and arrogant personalities offend potential sensitive lovers, their proclivity to cheat destroys the trust necessary for any loving relationship and their insatiable desire only leaves their partners feeling unworthy and empty.

On the other side, as Tricia got to know Henry, her naturally aggressive nature became more pensive because she thought he knew things she did not. She was particularly interested in his knowledge of philosophy—she had never known a philosopher. She began asking him many questions that often turned into ranging, deep and provocatively probing conversations that occasionally shook her sensibilities.

Characteristically, Tricia began one conversation with an attack on men and what she called toxic masculinity. She said male patriarchy and hierarchy had subjected women for centuries, but this had changed under feminism, which made her a militant cultural feminist. Henry agreed women had been subjugated but pointed out that

Cleopatra had manipulated men and Ottoman Queen Theodora had been evil. He then pointed out that feminism had only arisen under democracy and its emphasis on equality, which does not exist in nature. Henry continued and said history tells us democracies are rare and usually short, which could mean the end of feminism. Tricia got angry and said women will never be subjugated again, to which Henry said hopefully so, but he then asked Tricia to compare her life with a traditional non-feminist woman. Most traditional women are honored by men and have husbands, children and a family, whereas feminists have lost any special place of honor in men's minds, are considered competitors and are usually without the husbands, children and families so desperately wanted. He asked authentic five Tricia if she was loved, and now, uncharacteristically pensive, she looked at Henry for a long time, not sure what to say.

After a bit Tricia went off again like a firecracker on morality. She excoriated capitalism, greed and the unwillingness to help the poor. Excitedly she exclaimed that the poor have rights to food and shelter and said not providing that is immoral. Now mildly amused, Henry said that feminists and most of contemporary America has adopted the assassin's moral creed, which says that if nothing is true everything is permitted. Under it, capitalistic ambition has become greed, reward for effort has become socialism's from each their ability, the ethic of work is now to each their need, Locke and Jefferson's negative rights have become positive rights imposing obligations taking others' rights, Bentham's serpent-winding utilitarianism has superseded Hobbes's social contract, the freedom everyone used to fight for has become empty and equal in all respects, utterly ignoring Darwin and Malthus's *Essay Concerning Human Population*. Now pensive Tricia listened as Henry concluded saying, "Your ungrounded morality now permits almost anything, like easy no-fault divorce, unrestrained sexuality, ubiquitous violence, adolescent youth rioters and crime that is always society's fault and not the criminal's. Again, Tricia just looked at Henry quizzically.

Tricia then became uncharacteristically quiet and, to Henry's surprise, frank and vulnerable. She said she had been raised in an ambitious family in which graduating from an Ivy League school, becoming a professional, succeeding and getting rich were the only things that counted. She said she had done all of that but now felt empty and then quietly revealed she wanted a traditional family with a husband and children. Understanding Henry paused for some time and then said slowly, "I think your feminist and moral beliefs have taken that from you. Men want a dimorphic character and not a competitive one like themselves, so they rarely fall in love with or marry women of your type. Even if they do the lack of respect they get as a man and father quickly destroys any existing love, so your type is also usually divorced. Further, your wayward assassin's morality has weakened the rare special bond between man-husband-father and woman-wife-mother and shredded the moral norms that supported these natural roles and resulting families. Monogamy and heterosexuality have given way to a smorgasbord of unrestrained licentiousness including pornography, promiscuity, homosexuality, lesbianism, bisexuality and the transgender sex. You are hopelessly seeking a historic family in an increasing family-less new world." Henry was sorry to see Tricia look despondent.

Now thoughtful, Tricia said she was unhappy and asked Henry why. Henry said, "Happiness is an elusive state, so we need to understand it before I can answer your question. Ancient philosopher Aristotle thought happiness consists in a life well lived in accordance with virtue and accompanied by a moderate possession of external goods. Another philosopher Boethius thought happiness was avoiding desire and seeking a condition of self-sufficiency with no wants. Other philosophers believed happiness comes from being worthy of respect and joyful." Henry added that he thought true love can also foster happiness but not always. With that Henry said, "There could be many reasons for your unhappiness, but I suspect it is your character type that makes you so," which stunned Tricia.

Henry said, "Nothing is true in your relative morality, which makes for unrealistic expectations that never satisfy your desires, including your desire for love. The truth is that nature is easily satisfied, and it is your insatiable desire that makes you unhappy, bereft of fulfillment, full of remorse and loveless. You are the kind of person always thinking you will be happy if you were there, but when you get there you are still unhappy because it is now here. Conversely, philosophers have written, 'Blessed is the person who expects nothing, for they shall never be disappointed.' People are rich in proportion to the things they don't want, and a person cannot lose what they never had. The simple truth is you will never be happy wanting more—true happiness resides in appreciating what you have now and not some future unknown, which includes love.

As Eros, I watched Tricia, now upset and vacillating between hurt and remorse, angrily say to Henry, "I don't see you with a woman lover and then assert that she was capable of love." It was sad to watch; I have seen it so many times with loveless authentic five personalities. Tricia's type is too unstable, desirous, seeking and preoccupied with self to love and be happy. Her type is never satisfied and is always seeking more of the love they do not have. It is like faux love on steroids going haywire, never having enough. Tricia is the kind of personality, when married, that is never satisfied with their spouse and is always seeking another who is younger, smarter, richer or better looking. Her type is incapable of understanding that there are no perfect spouses, so just replacing them for a better one does not bring love or happiness. This is why I mentioned earlier that Tricia's character rarely leads to

love and is usually divorced and unhappy and always tragic. Indeed, it was Henry himself who wrote her epitaph
when he said he could never love a difficult, desire-driven,
pushy feminist.

CHAPTER SEVEN

Empty Anonymous Love

After her conversation with Henry, Tricia reluctantly realized that Henry did not want her and was horrified by the thought that, because of her personality type, no man may ever want her. With that their relationship naturally faded into history and became just one of those past love experiences that exist in people's memories.

Back in Portland circumstances were brewing that would soon engulf Henry in a web of temptation and deceit. After their painful break up in high school, Ann Miller had drifted rather aimlessly through life. She had gone to the University of Oregon for a year, married a townie who looked like her father, got pregnant, had two daughters, divorced, moved back to Portland and found a waitress job. Because she could not make ends meet she moved back with her parents when she started dating Clew Lewson, who was a close friend of her old boyfriend Ryan Peterson.

Unbeknownst to her at the time, her relationship with Clew was fated to happen. Her type two unauthentic character strangely meshed well with Clew, who was Heidegger's anonymous one. Those are people who are only in their heads and not in this world; they are shallow, self-absorbed and preoccupied with the present. With these characteristics, Clew was incapable of long-term, sustained, intimate relationships, incompetent with money and unable to grow beyond level-two desire love. Indeed, Ann found sex with Clew much like the shaking hands found in low-level gratification love. I will describe Clew's character more shortly but for now the important point is that Clew had asked Ann to marry him, and Ann was struggling to decide.

She found many aspects of Clew's persona exciting, but she still loved Henry, and his loss still pained her. She was unsure what to do, so she went to her mother Ellen and asked her advice. The first thing she did was to ask her if she loved Henry, and she said yes. Ann's mother said, "Then go to him now!" Stunned into reality, Ann drove to Henry's mother's house to find out where Henry was. Eleanor welcomed her like an old friend, and Ann explained her problem, which quickly put Eleanor in a conundrum. On one hand she knew Ann had hurt her son deeply, but on the other she saw a young woman herself hurt and seeking love. She knew her son was strong and thought Ann needed help, so she gave her his address in New York. Ann went straight home, packed her bags, went to the airport, flew to New York and took a cab to Henry's apartment.

Henry was taking a shower when she rang the bell, and when he opened the door in a towel, Ann was startled, looking at a buff and handsome half-naked man. She did not recognize the thin and gangly Henry she had known, so she assumed this was his roommate. She asked if Henry Phillips was in, to which Henry, who recognized her and was amused, said yes. Uncomfortably attracted, Ann tried not to look at Henry who just sat back and smiled. After a bit she got nervous and asked again if Henry was home, to which Henry again said yes. Perplexed, Ann studied Henry's face and noticed the small scar on his forehead that she had accidently given him with a baseball bat when they were young. She suddenly realized it was Henry. She spontaneously ran and hugged him and said, "I am so happy you have grown into such a handsome man! The two hugged and kissed for some time before the bedroom."

With their reunion, Ann and Henry's relationship partially rekindled. Ann felt happy thinking she had regained the man she loved, which stabilized her personality and gradually her personal life. Henry was a little confused.

On one hand it felt good to have regained the friendship of a lost old friend, but on the other he was wary of her former disloyalty and closely guarded his heart. He was wary of falling in love again with Ann, so he kept up a guard to his citadel.

Henry had had enough of New York and decided he had learned enough from Silicon Equities to start his own business, so with Ann he piled his possessions in a U-Haul and moved back to Portland. He rented a cheap apartment in a low-cost southeast neighborhood and moved in with Ann. With the little money he had saved, he rented a small office space, bought some office furniture and equipment, registered Phillips Securities with the Corporation Division and started working like a madman on a mission, hoping fortune would favor his bravery.

Portland had dramatically changed since Henry's youth. It was no longer made up of conservative farmers and industrious businessmen. The leading clubs like the Racquet Club, University Club and Multnomah Athletic Club had faded, the pristine Pacific air was gone because of global warming and forest fires and the zeitgeist was chaotic disorder. Because of global warming there had been massive fires in California and Oregon, making parts of California uninhabitable and Portland's Air Quality Index sometimes 350 rather than 10, which had caused many of those crazy left-leaning gold seekers to move north. Henry learned they had usurped state government and monopolized urban areas like Portland and Eugene.

Their new policies had changed Portland's landscape. They had abandoned vagrancy and loitering laws and declared homelessness society's problem; the result was a city awash with vagrants and tents. In their zeal to care for these henceforth unseen citizens, they set up free kitchens and shelters, which only brought more of them—these new liberals never heard of Thomas Malthus's truism: the more need you feed the more need you get. There was garbage, human waste and drug needles everywhere. The worst were the riots every evening in downtown Portland. Some citizens had begun to protest against what they considered police brutality, but gradually their peaceful evening vigils were usurped by roving, black-clad, unemployed irresponsible and destructive young people. They fought with police, painted graffiti everywhere, smashed windows, started fires, blocked roads, attacked drivers and tore down statues of Abraham Lincoln, Thomas Jefferson and even a beloved elk. They called themselves anti-fascists but were really out of control lawless hoodlums. The new liberal leadership, led by Democratic mayor Tim Weller, lacked the political will to enforce the law and bring about order, and rather than support Portland's police force, he undermined and defunded them.

These socialist minded new political leaders had also started alienating Portland's business base with increasing anti-commerce legislation and high taxes. As a result many businesses had left Oregon and most abandoned the now graffiti-marred, plywood-fronted former stores of downtown Portland. It had become a quasi-wasteland with few businesspeople during the day and roaming homeless and police-baiting, rioting youth during the night.

Henry wondered what had gone wrong…why there was so much disorder, political strife and violence. One day at work Henry made a call on someone he had been told is both rich and a power broker in Portland. He was a little nervous when he walked into Bill Huffy's office and asked the receptionist if he could see him in order to describe his company and discuss securities. After a bit he was waved into Mr. Huffy's office. Huffy was a small, wiry man about sixty years old with darting and penetrating eyes. He reminded Henry of Lenin.

After discussing securities he asked Huffy about politics because he had been told that he was the moving force in the Democratic Party, the silent power behind the throne and king maker. He was the one who pulled all the political strings in Portland and Oregon. Huffy was initially wary but quickly started bragging about his party's progressive accomplishments. He said Portland used to be run by a bunch of backward bumpkins until he came. He said after settling in Portland he immediately recruited charismatic Nell Goldenberg to run for mayor, brokered the liberal Newtown newspaper chain purchase of the moribund *Oregonian*, recruited Eastern ultra-liberal Eckert Mack to rewrite the history of Portland from the liberal perspective and over time brought political leaders like Gen Kafary, Eugenia Took and Portland mayors Simon Damer and Tim Weller to leadership positions.

Huffy then, in Rousseauian fashion, bragged that his progressive party had been responsible for placing much of the blame for individual problems on society, had decriminalized many former crimes and dramatically increased taxes on businesses. He said he had kicked the old boy bureaucracy out and created a progressive force that brought a new code elevating social justice within a multicultural environment. He said one of the reasons he had left his hometown of Chicago was because it was a city in serious decline with racial, infrastructure and police problems, losing industrial jobs mostly due to the old boy network that ran it.

The source of Portland's issues became crystal clear to Henry; he got pissed and inveighed hard on a very surprised Bill Huffy. He said, "I am a fourth generation Oregonian who has lived in Portland most of my life, and I can assure you that my city was far better off under those old 'backward bumpkin' boys than your ugly liberal amorphous vapor of sentimentality where everything is decided capriciously by feelings." Henry laid in and said, "It is your collectivism that has ruined personal responsibility and accountability, which has been a major source of our homeless problem; it is your lack of support for the police and unwillingness to prosecute wrongdoers that has caused the crime and rioting problems we now face; it is your socialistic regulations and high taxes on businesses that have brought fewer businesses, higher unemployment, less tax revenue and the need for more money; it is your wayward party's focus on identity politics that has abandoned our traditional melting pot theory and brought racial tension. No, Mr. Duffy, the real problem is you and your party, which, under your leadership, is ruining my Portland just like it did Chicago!"

Huffy was stunned and obviously irritated, and he began stammering and stuttering trying to explain his position, but Henry just kept at him. It turned out Huffy was a bag of wind unable to give a direct answer to a direct question, and his responses were always vague and tenuous because he feared he might be shown wrong. He would usually avoid facts and principles and turn to emotionally driven, often non-syllogistic and evasive metaphors to try and make a point. Because his world outlook was subjective, Henry often backed him into a contradiction, to which he would always say, "It's complicated." Henry had learned long ago that anyone who says that it's complicated does not understand the problem, has no clear vision, is confused and does not know what to do.

I mentioned in the beginning how intangibles in life like politics, civil strife and class affect how we love, and Huffy's Portland demonstrates how this plays out in reality. Hardball politics only breed distrust, which brings wariness of love; the desire for power, which becomes more important than who or what we love; chronic anger, which blocks out tenderness and the desire for love; and a society imbued with disarray and caprice, which makes people indulge their own appetites rather than be other regarding and encourages wayward personalities like the anonymous one, who I will describe next. I have already described how Constance Worthington's class snobbery ended Betsy and Henry's budding love affair. Needless to say, after their conversation Huffy did not give Henry any business and condescendingly asked him to leave.

Clew Lewson, the man who had asked Ann to marry him, is an example of Heidegger's anonymous personality described in Henry's book *Unauthentic, Authentic and Anonymous Character Types and Love*. I will describe his type here because it is the type that thrives under Portland's chaotic conditions, and I will show how it manifests in love with Ann later. Anonymous types are empty nabobs of value to no one and are utterly incapable of anything beyond desire love because they are so selfish. They view others like a hammer or utensil to be used as an object, thus depriving others of their existential freedom, viewing others to be used, such as for sex, which makes one component of love, authentic communication, impossible. Instead, they spend their love lives bounding between infatuation and desire, love never satisfied.

Anonymous ones like Clew follow convention, take on mechanical habits, are characterized by averageness and retreat from personal commitment and responsible decision. They fear commitment and the demands of love. They appear strong and self-reliant but in reality are weak and utterly reliant on others for any sense of self. Heidegger described their condition as fallenness because they lose themselves in their present preoccupations and indulge in novelty and simple momentary distractions that make them unable to achieve authentic understanding. They are always looking for someone better, which makes them disloyal and incapable of true love. They have restricted world horizons and down deep are cowards retreating from life.

All of this makes anonymous ones quite miserable. They go through life as selfish, invisible, leveled and reduced beings who have forfeited their unique probabilities. On top of this they are usually poor, inadequate providers for families, divorced and alone without loved ones.

Back at Oxford, Professor Steve Harper was giving his usual lecture on Kierkegaard and Heidegger when he absentmindedly said that one of his former students had written a well-known book on their character types and love. The class became instantly interested and started asking the professor, who suddenly realized he had made a huge blunder, which student it was. It did not take the students long to compare the publication date of the book with Professor Harper's students at that time, and within an hour Henry's name was spread across social media as the author and he became famous overnight. Henry's co-workers were astonished, Tricia was amazed, his mother phoned and he started getting calls from publishers, agents and television shows asking for appearances. Henry took it with poise but never quite got over the loss of his privacy.

Ann, who had been harboring thoughts about Henry, was also amazed at his success and fame and decided now was the time. This is painful for me to relate because it involves so much disappointment, rejection and pain, but this is often what happens to unauthentic people. Ann waited until the evening when she and Henry were alone and after a few glasses of wine asked Henry to marry her. She said she had always loved him and wanted to start a family with him. She was stunned by Henry's silence—she was hurtfully reminded that he did not want her. She listened quietly as Henry said he had always valued their friendship, but she was not the kind of person with whom he could fall deeply in love, be married or have a family. With that Ann ran from the house sobbing.

Henry had struggled to make the relationship with Ann work, but there were too many obstacles. Her shallow personality and lack of loyalty were barriers to any deep, authentic love relationship—he just did not want her. Ann's reaction was first pain and then anger at being rejected, which gradually turned into self-destructive behavior. In revenge she sought out the man who had asked her to marry him, Clew Lewson, and revived their relationship. Shallow Clew was flattered with the attention. To Ann's dismay, it was more of the same shallow affair—mostly physical, sex was again empty like shaking hands, the lust got old fast and the same deep unsatisfied desire reemerged. Ann felt the same feeling she had felt back in high school when she went out with Ryan Peterson—she again felt she had lost the right man and was with the wrong man. After a short time together in Portland, Ann and Clew took off for a warmer climate in Southern California.

Henry felt differently. He felt no jealousy, and down deep he thought they were a match and hoped Ann would find happiness. He decided to put his head down and focus on his business and Portland's political problems. First, however, he got the surprise of his life.

Henry was about to experience a form of love that transcends personality type and is invariably level-three love in spite of any discord. It was a Saturday morning when Henry answered a knock on his door only to see a rather handsome young man looking at him earnestly. After a bit he haltingly said that his name was John Brown, his mother was Vicki Brown and he believed Henry was his father. Henry was speechless and asked him to come in—he had long forgotten his trysts with Vicki in order to impregnate her. John said his parents divorced long ago and that his mother had died of cancer recently. Just before she died, she had told fifteen-year-old John about his real father and suggested he go find him because he had nobody else in the world.

Henry was amazed watching him talk. John looked very much like him with his dark hair, fair complexion and height. He noticed his bold and brave character and obvious intelligence. He clearly was an authentic personality like himself. John said he had no place to go or people to see and asked if he could stay. Henry said of course and immediately showed him a room, and with that, Henry had a son. It was the beginning of a very special and unique loving relationship between a parent and child that lasted for the rest of Henry's life.

Henry's securities business was thriving due to his perseverance and hard work, and he was getting rich. He had lived in apartments most of his life, so he decided it was time to buy a real house. He hired a broker and spent a lot of time looking at moderate to nice houses, but none seemed to turn him on. On a lark, his broker took him one day to visit the Williams Estate, which had been languishing on the market for some time. Henry was immediately taken with the old English style house, extensive lawn and gardens, pool and tennis court. He was particularly taken with the mahogany library that could hold all of his books. They had been asking $5 million for the estate, Henry took a deep breath and offered $3 million; they settled at $3.5 million and closed the deal. It was an exciting day for Henry moving into his new grand home with John, who got a new room of his own.

It had been a tumultuous time in Henry's life with the loss of Betsy, strife in Portland, chaotic love life with Tricia and Ann and now a son he did not consider he had. But his life was about to change for the better.

CHAPTER EIGHT

True Love

After he had settled into his new house, Henry told his mother it was time she sold her old house and move in with him and John. Eleanor was excited to live with her son and grandson in a beautiful house where she had her own extensive suite, bathroom and kitchen—happily she joined the growing household. Henry enrolled John in a local private high school and special classes designed to prepare him for college. He would often take John to the office in order for him to learn the securities business. John was intrigued with the business, learned it easily and spent summers working as an agent in the company. Over time, Henry and John's relationship deepened. At thirty-five years old, Henry felt good living with his family in his new home while slowly growing Phillips Securities and expanding into new markets. Within a few years he had established offices in most major American cities and was beginning to move into some overseas markets.

Henry was happy, but deep down there was something missing. He often found himself thinking about Betsy and wondering what she was doing. He imagined she had married some aristocratic prince and was living in some fancy country home surrounded by children, so he was surprised one day when he got a letter from Phillip Worthington describing her circumstances. Initially the letter was warm and chatty but quickly got down to his reason for writing, which was to tell Henry that Betsy was miserable. She had been pursued by a number of eligible men, none of whom interested her; she had gained a reputation as a tease and had given up seeking love and marriage. He said she spent most of her time at her parents' alone. Phillip admitted that his artificial class world was empty and his mother's prohibiting their marriage was wrong, but it was just the way things are. He closed the letter rather philosophically, resigned to Betsy's unfortunate fate.

The letter tugged at Henry's heart but also confused him. Why is he being told this when it was Betsy and her mother who had refused his marriage proposal. At dinner that night, Henry told his mother and son the whole story about Betsy and the letter he had just received when unexpectedly the doorbell rang. When Henry opened it he was shocked to see a serious looking Constance Worthington, who asked if she could talk with him. She said she had traveled from England to tell him she had taken some "physic, pomp!" and was most unhappy seeing her daughter so miserably distraught. She said she had made a mistake weighing Betsy down with stifling social conventions and making her date men she found weak, delicate and effeminate. Constance paused, looked long and hard at Henry, and finally said that she had been wrong, her daughter loved him and that she was sorry. She asked Henry if he would be willing to go see Betsy; he did not respond but knew what needed to be done.

The next day back at Oxford, Harold Worthington was walking by Betsy's room when he heard soft crying, so he went in and saw his daughter red-eyed, curled up on her bed. He knew the reason and said to Betsy, "If you love that man, you need to go and get him now—pack and I will drive you to the airport." Suddenly animated, Betsy agreed, hugged her dad and quickly packed a few things. Just as they were about to leave the doorbell rang and in walked an intent looking Henry. Betsy and Harold were stunned when Henry said, "I don't give a god damn about your social conventions, all I know is that I love this woman and I am taking her home with me now!" Harold smiled and said, "She's yours," and Betsy flew to Henry's arms, kissed him long and hard and buried her head in his chest. After a long embrace, Henry picked up Betsy's suitcase, said goodbye to Harold, took Betsy by the hand to the car, drove to the airport and flew back to Portland with the love of his life. Both Henry and Betsy were brimming with joy and anticipation as they winged their way to Portland together.

It was like life was settling the way it should. Betsy became close friends with Eleanor and John, got to know the house and staff, including Alice the housekeeper and Marcos the gardener, and gradually Henry's friends and business associates. She felt happy living with such a successful author and businessman in a beautiful house. Henry and Betsy's deep feelings for each other quickly flooded back, and their relationship flourished. As two authentic-four people they were on the verge of achieving rare grade-four love.

To appreciate grade-four love, recall the limitations of the lower grades described earlier. The lowest was the fleeting infatuation of Ryan and Clew and the next-level Ann's insatiable desire-driven transient love due to insecurity and self-loathing. Henry never felt comfortable in love with Ann due to these characteristics, but that was about to change dramatically with Betsy. Unlike Ann, as an authentic person Betsy had the self-confidence to experience the true love Henry was ready for. It happened spontaneously without outside influence. It started with deep affection, fondness, warmth, intimacy, devotion and adoration for each other. It was an unconditional love in which they lost themselves to a higher constant affection for the other—a kind of timeless, stable and unobscure love irrespective of their place and time—they were raised above the accidents of the present. They were entering the shrine of true love free from envy, boasting, arrogance, irritability and resentment. It is a kind of love that just naturally occurs between people who love themselves first, and desire has become contentment. Sex is no longer satisfying hormonally driven desire, a state many never transcend, but rather done for the higher purpose of re-production. Henry and Betsy's love's stars were aligning.

One significant alignment came when they reconciled kindness and justice. Recall that Betsy favored kindness and Henry justice and that each had misinterpreted the other's sentiment. Betsy had interpreted Henry's courtesy as kindness, whereas for Henry it was really due to a sense of justice. I was concerned that this unmet expectation of theirs could kill their budding love. What happened is their love began breaking down their hard shell of ego, which brought happiness and an expansive and generous attitude toward each other. So, when they discovered this difference, their solution was not recrimination but rather understanding. Henry learned that kindness comes from justice and Betsy that kindness sometimes must be tempered by justice. They learned from each other that people have a greater chance to flourish in life if they are both kind and just.

It was a happy household with Betsy, Henry, Eleanor and John, and it did not take long for Henry to propose marriage. They had a grand wedding with all of Betsy's relatives, and within a month Betsy was pregnant. It was a pleasure for me to watch two authentic people in true love bringing new life into the world—over the next ten years Betsy and Henry filled the house with five noisy children, all of whom had Betsy's red hair. Little did they know how the awful turn of events would affect them.

CHAPTER NINE

Love and Fate

It was a happy growing household that brought Peter, James, Amy, Henry and Kathy into the world. The house was littered with toys, diapers and little ones scampering everywhere. Eleanor was a doting grandmother and John an avuncular step-brother. As the children grew, the family took innumerable trips camping in the mountains, hiking the coast or swimming in some lake or the house pool, always singing. Holidays were special and in particular Christmas when they would decorate the biggest tree they could find and have a mountain of presents to open.

John, who had changed his last name to Phillips, grew into a handsome, cultured and mannered man who worshiped his father. He had followed his father to Oxford and entered the family securities business, where he had risen to a vice president. He had a warm relationship with Betsy and Eleanor and was close to his step-brothers and sisters, intimate with his father Henry and was busy dating young women, looking for a life mate.

Henry had watched with dismay as his beloved Portland had slipped further and further over time into chaos—it was like all the original problems times ten. Everywhere there was graffiti, abandoned damaged cars, broken windows, defaced public monuments, blocked off streets, fires and pervasive homelessness, with tents along with garbage and human waste. Downtown had become an abandoned wasteland that businesses had long ago fled due to the nightly looting, vandalism and roaming violent youths. The infrastructure had crumbled, and the roads were pot-holed.

But by far the worst problem was the increased violence. In addition to carjacking, mugging and fights, there were nightly riots and almost constant shootings. Portland had become a very dangerous place to be at night due to one of the highest murder rates in America. The reduced police force was overwhelmed with calls, and many areas of the city had become lawless, ruled only by gangs or volatile vigilantism. It was like nobody was at the helm trying to steer the ship to a safe port—it was like nobody cared.

Henry was so angered by Portland's inept leadership he decided one night to go to a city council meeting. He found a seat in the back and watched long-time Mayor Tim Weller, council member Lew Day and political kingpin Bill Huffy discussing what to do. Their comments were so vacuous and inept that Henry was about to say something when this strong and forceful stentorian voice rose from the crowd and lambasted the council. It was Henry Fielding, Portland's leading industrialist and largest employer. Henry was mesmerized with his forceful arguments, trenchant accusations and boldness. He also thought there was something strangely familiar about Mr. Fielding's looks, bearing and personality, which intrigued him.

Henry was emboldened by Fielding's remarks, so he interrupted him and started lecturing the council himself, focusing on Bill Huffy. Huffy went stone quiet because he knew Henry was a famous author and forceful anti-liberal voice. With Henry Fielding watching, Henry accused Huffy, the mayor, the entire city council and the long string of past Democratic mayors of being incompetent. They had brought machine politics and liberal political views such as defunding police, tolerated lawlessness, decriminalized drugs and non-prosecution of criminals. They jejunely replace traditional policing with community policing and then are dismayed when it does not work. The only answer to the continuing violence is "things are too far downstream," which means you could have fixed the things that made the criminals but because of human nature they can never quite fix those sources so the violence continues. They had lost any appreciation for law and order and thus no longer had the will to enforce the law, which was a major source of Portland's problems. With their groundless, free-floating social justice all problems had become society's problems and not the individual's. Their liberal bent had focused them so much on meeting need they had taken for granted business enterprise that paid the taxes that paid for the services they wanted to give. Ironically, because most businesses had abandoned downtown, there was less tax revenue and services for the poor. To make up the difference they raided other sources of income, such as the water bureau's budget, as well as diverted money to pet projects such as former mayor Simon Damer's bike lanes, leaving no money to maintain the decaying roads.

Henry then took aim at Duffy and said, "You came to our wonderful city from Chicago, which you left because of its machine politics and loss of industrial jobs. Well, it is people like you who screwed up Chicago, and now you have done it to Portland—now Portland has machine politics and loss of jobs. It is you and those like you who are the problem." Duffy winced, but Henry was not done. It is your assassin's creed philosophy—when everything is relative nothing is true—that makes everything permitted which is exactly what we see in Portland today. Your bleeding hearts have made decisions based on feelings, so your compassion is unrestrained and out of control—you have become empty, confused and impotent maudlin leaders unsure what to do next. Your utilitarian consequentialist ethics has ignored causes and only massages problems but never solves them.

Henry then said to Huffy and the stunned council that their vision of America was un-American because it was so foreign to the Founding Fathers' intentions. "The Founding Fathers wanted small government, and you have brought big government; they wanted unobtrusive government, and you want government to control all aspects of citizens' lives; they wanted low taxation, and you have brought high taxation; they wanted no federal income tax, and you brought it with the Sixteenth Amendment; they wanted states' rights, and you want to limit them; they wanted the federal government to control only interstate commerce, and you have expanded it to include intrastate commerce; they wanted low debt, and you have brought us high, unsustainable debt; they eschewed socialism, and you embrace it; and they did not want to encumber future generations, whereas you do under a mythical sacred pact between generations.

Henry forcefully concluded to a silent chamber, "It was you, Mr. Huffy, and those like you who have brought incivility, intolerance and contention to my beloved Portland, which has destroyed any civic feelings of fraternity, respect and love." With that Henry left the chamber but on the way out was stopped by Henry Fielding, who said, "Well done."

Because love is often a swift shadow that never runs smoothly, some have avoided it altogether due to its unpredictability. Betsy and Henry were happily in love, but circumstances beyond their control adumbrated problems. Certainly, there were occasional disagreements mostly over politics—Betsy was liberal and sympathized with the downtown protestors, and Henry was conservative and thought they were violent rogue youths that should be punished. Betsy was focused on bringing justice, and Henry with restoring order. One day Betsy made the fateful decision to go downtown and try and do what she could to help the protestors and stop the rioting. Henry tried unsuccessfully to dissuade her from going, so he went with her gingerly, avoiding the violence and keeping Betsy out of trouble. Believing she was helping, Betsy became a regular, until late one night Henry got a call from the police saying that she had been arrested and was in jail. Alarmed, Henry quickly went to see her and discovered she was in serious trouble.

Betsy had been arrested for murder. The federal police, along with the federal prosecutor, showed Henry a video of Betsy holding a Molotov cocktail that had been thrown and killed two federal police officers. There was also an eye witness who said they saw Betsy throw the cocktail at the police, and her fingerprints were all over some of the remaining shards of glass. The timing could not have been worse because the federal agents were looking for an excuse to prosecute someone for the violence, so they indicted Betsy. Henry hired the best criminal attorney he could and they fought the allegations in court for months, but in the end she was sentenced to twenty years to life in jail. Henry was stunned as the bailiffs lead solemn, handcuffed Betsy away to the federal penitentiary.

In a very short span, everyone's lives were changed. Betsy was off to prison, Henry was now a lone parent, their children missed their mother, Eleanor and John were dismayed and Betsy's mother, father, sister and brother were devastated. The big house went cold and quiet. After a week or so Henry went to see Betsy before they transferred her to the federal prison. It was a final, wrenching goodbye; Betsy said to Henry that he must forget her, move on in life and care for the children who will need a new mother. Crying she said to Henry, "I release you from any obligations," and turned and left. Distraught Henry went home to decide what to do.

CHAPTER TEN

Love and Hate

Henry was now forty-five years old, had lived a full and varied life and had loved and been loved. He felt fortunate to have a family, successful business and home. He had enjoyed when he could and now must endure what he has; but he decided he needed a break in life—he needed to get away for a while to sort things out and settle his mind. He talked with Eleanor, John and his children, and they all encouraged him to take some time off. So, Henry turned over the reins of Phillips Securities to John, entrusted the care of his children to Eleanor and Constance Worthington, who moved in to help, packed his bags and headed out to Eastern Oregon in his old Jeep.

Henry felt good driving through wide open eastern Oregon away from the pressures of business and memory of Betsy. Henry was a city boy—he was born in the city, grew up in the city and lived in it all his life, so rural America was engagingly foreign. He drove through large and small towns like Bend and Burns and one very small stop—Frenchglen—that seemed to herald the end of civilization. Driving along the Alvord Desert on the eastern slope of the Steens Mountains, he saw some people in a field harvesting crops. He thought that would be a vigorous job close to nature that would be good for him, so he took the next driveway and drove into the Jordan Valley Ranch. He asked to see the foreman and was taken to Jacob Hefty, a large, heavyset man with piercing eyes whose mere presence commanded respect and obedience. Jacob asked Henry what he wanted and Henry said a job, which surprised Jacob because he was obviously not the kind of man to be a ranch hand. However, Henry was in good shape and he needed a hand for harvesting the alfalfa, so he showed him a room and said see you at five in the morning.

So began a new chapter in Henry's life, working on the Jordan Valley Ranch as a field hand for $10 per day. It was a robust experience that Henry quickly took to—he was up at five, had a large breakfast in the cook shack with the other hands and was bucking hay in the field by six thirty. The workers were an eclectic mix of older, long-time grizzled employees with skin like leather, some strong teenage boys from Burns earning money during the summer, a few buckaroos who spent most of their time on horses looking after cows and a scattering of hardened ex-convicts. After one particularly violent fight between two of them at dinner, Henry quickly learned that the cons should be avoided. It was hard, taxing work in very hot weather, but Henry enjoyed the dry heat, juniper and sagebrush smell, rugged Steens Mountains and isolation. After months of hard physical work and meat and mashed potatoes, Henry became quite strong, fit and healthy.

The nature of love was the last thing on Henry's mind when he met the ranch owner's daughter Martha Wilson at a picnic they had for the employees. She was about forty, a well-built and handsome woman with long blonde hair that she usually wore in a bun; she was oddly sexy in a strange way. They struck up an easy conversation during which Henry was attracted to her earthy, sophisticated, worldly and knowledgeable cowgirl persona. Martha found Henry interesting and handsome, but he did not look, sound or act like a ranch hand, so she asked who he was. With that Henry told her of his family back in Portland and loss of Betsy. Martha suddenly and excitedly exclaimed that she had read about him, that he was the author of the famous book on character types and love, which she had read, and that he was the owner of Phillips Securities! She asked what on earth he was doing working in the fields on their ranch. Henry smiled and said he wanted a break from civilization, was enjoying the hard work and solitude and would appreciate it if she would keep it to herself. Aghast, Martha said, "Of course."

Henry and Martha spent much time together over the months talking about everything, and their relationship deepened. It was a different kind of relationship between opposite sexes who found each other appealing but strangely bereft of any romantic love or sexual attraction. At first Henry was perplexed until one night Martha said that like ancient Sappho of Lesbos she was a lesbian. She said she liked men and loved her father and brother but did not find men sexually appealing. She said they were too rough and hard and she was attracted to the soft bodies of women. She said she found the smell of male testosterone revolting. She was living at the ranch because she was tired of society's rejections and disapprobation and because she had a lover who was a waitress at the café in Denio.

Curious, Henry asked her if she had any maternal feelings to procreate children, and Martha said yes, but not with a man. She said she planned on marrying her lover and adopting children. She also mentioned the future possibility of harvesting the chromosomes from her lover to fertilize one of her ova. She said I know you may find me odd, but this is my nature—it is the way God made me. As an afterthought she looked at Henry and said, "If I was interested in men, you should know you would be the one." Henry smiled and said thanks and that her sexual orientation did not bother him at all. Indeed, he told her he thought she was his fourth kind of authentic person, which thrilled Martha. He said you are stable, confident, have self-esteem, are somewhat detached, endeavor to be happy and are living life on your own terms. With that, Henry and Martha's platonic relationship deepened.

Let me make one final comment on Martha's lesbianism when it comes to love. Zeus does not make everyone perfect—everyone has some form of defect. Martha's just happened to be a different kind of harmless sexual orientation that a small percentage of all populations have had over the ages. Indeed, I have noticed that these different kinds of people can be the most authentic and able to achieve higher forms of love. Many fall in love with and marry those who they want and not who others want, they know who they are compatible with, they seek true love, when they find the one they love they commit themselves and they think they are worthy of love, which makes them loveable. It may sound odd to you, but Martha's lesbianism enabled her to achieve true love.

There is a continuum from love to loathing with many intermediate emotional states. Henry had experienced the highest forms of true love with Betsy and witnessed it with Martha, and now he was about to experience the opposite—pure, unadulterated hate. He had always known that rural Oregonians, those that live in small towns, despise liberal city folk, but he had never experienced the depth of it firsthand. One weekend Henry drove to Burns to do some shopping. As he turned one corner downtown he saw a very large, boisterous crowd at the county court-house, so out of curiosity he parked and went over to see what was going on. On the podium was an elderly, rather thin, grey-haired gentleman denouncing big city liberal Democrats that were slowly sucking the life blood of small towns with their evil morality, punishing laws and high taxes, to the crowd's loud approval. He said those liberal enemies in Portland, Salem and Eugene care more about Black lives, sexual orientation, special education, homelessness and illegal foreigners than us hardworking, self-reliant farmers and ranchers who are trying to survive in the country. He exclaimed, "We work to grow crops and raise cattle that are sent to these ugly pits of slime, and they return the favor by passing environmental and restrictive land use laws that make it harder for us to do our jobs and survive!" After the crowd's roar of approval had died down he then said, "These city slickers can't control crime and violence in their own cities and are socialists who give the poor free handouts but let us country folk starve while many of them live in luxury." Looking around, Henry saw a sea of angry red faces armed to the teeth with Lugers and AK-47s itching for rebellion and violence.

Shaken, Henry went to a nearby restaurant for lunch where he saw more angry people and signs that said *We do not serve liberal Democrats here, City people are not welcome*, and *It's time to secede from Oregon*. Shortly the man who had been speaking entered with a group of people and sat at the table next to him. Henry could overhear them talking rabidly about secession and a separate state; organizing vigilante posses; keeping the Bureau of Land Management, state police, FBI and IRS tax collectors out; and assassination of some state leaders. Suddenly the man became aware of Henry, and everyone went silent when he asked who he was. Thinking his life could be over soon Henry looked the man square in the eye and said he was a Portlander who was disgusted with the leadership of his city, so he was working at the Jordan Valley Ranch as a ranch hand. The man stared long and hard at Henry and then broke into loud laughter, saying he likes people who tell it straight and despise big city liberal leaders. He said his name was Mark Finicus, and with that the two began a long-ranging conversation. Henry described Bill Huffy and his debate with him along with the chaos in Portland, and Mark told Henry about the BLM voiding his grazing permits, his loss of cattle and subsequent money problems and how the IRS seized his ranch and the state police evicted him. Mark was a very angry man full of hate who was out for revenge.

Mark described himself as a Jeffersonian Libertarian and launched into a demagogic tirade listing the reasons rural people hate urban people for the benefit of everyone in the café, including Henry. He said urbanites are erasing our true American heritage of self-reliance, individualism, freedom, limited government, low taxation, low debt, sacred traditions and family bonds. Angrily he said, "Those fuckers are bringing socialism and needy other-reliant people, collectivism and rule by government and slavery with their web of pernicious liberal laws. They are forever increasing our taxes and adding new ones to feed their bottomless need for money. There is less religion with their secularism, and traditions like saying the Lord's Prayer in school and celebrating Christmas are quickly vanishing. They dismembered our families with their emphasis on feminism, rainbow of sexual orientation and diminution of the role of fathers and restricted on our right to bear arms under the Second Amendment." Angrily he said, "Those liberal scum could care less about rural citizens' problems and deride us as unimportant flyover people." With his fist angrily punching the air he concluded that the revolution begins here and now: "We must secede from Oregon, and we must arm ourselves and kill those who try to stop us," which got a very long, loud cheer from the crowd.

Henry thought to himself that even though this man may be wild and a bit crazy, he does have some legitimate complaints, his words reveal a deep anger and hatred that is a cultural schism he doubted could ever be bridged, and someone was going to die soon. With that troubled Henry quietly left the café and drove back to the ranch.

Henry had had enough of rural ranch life and decided to get back into the mainstream. He was anxious to see his children but decided to go to New York first to see how his securities business was doing. He said goodbye to his Jordan Valley Ranch friends, drove to Boise and caught a flight to La Guardia. He had a cab drop him off at his branch office building, and he walked in wearing jeans and a T-shirt. The office was abuzz with activity with brokers in white shirts rushing everywhere when he asked to see the office manager. Shortly a very surprised young man appeared and said, "Mr. Phillips, it is an honor to have you here." He said his name was Jeremy Walker and he had worked in the San Francisco office. He'd seen Henry a few times when he visited although in a suit rather than jeans. Jeremy introduced the founder to all the astonished employees. Afterward, Henry asked Jeremy if he knew an attorney named Tricia Roberts. Jeremy said he knew the old Walker Law Firm but not Tricia and got its address for Henry.

When Henry arrived at Tricia's old law firm, the name had changed. He asked the receptionist if she knew where Tricia Roberts was and she said no, but another longtime attorney told him she had been disbarred. After some research, Henry finally found Tricia in a small, rundown apartment in a seedy part of New York—a far cry from her Fifth Avenue penthouse. Henry was shocked when she answered the door—she was dirty and disheveled, looked much older and had sores all over her face. Fully aware of her looks, Tricia was embarrassed, she said hi to Henry and let him in.

It was a profound and painful conversation with Tricia. She was glad to see Henry because he was an old friend and one of the few people who understood her.

With no pretense, she opened up to Henry and said, "It seems you were right, my authentic-five personality finally caught up with me. I have been disbarred, lost my firm, lost my job, lost my money, have been divorced numerous times and now live in this hellhole slowly killing myself with drugs. I have nothing worthy to show for my life other than wasted opportunities, lost loves, no children and a life of self-indulgence. Somehow the desire to be self-created and master my fate only brought me endless restlessness that resulted in wonton sensuality and debauchery." She cried and said, "I wish I could live my life again as a different person." Henry felt a great sense of compassion for Tricia; her hyper, aggressive, edgy and arrogant personality was gone, and she was living the denouement of her personality type in existential angst and anxiety. After a bit Henry hugged crying Tricia for a long time, kissed her forehead and said goodbye, thinking it would be the last time he would ever see her.

When Henry got back to his hotel there was an urgent message from John who told him his mother Eleanor had died from a stroke. Henry wasted no time, immediately returned to Portland to arrange a funeral for his mother, resume the presidency of Phillips Securities and care for his children Peter, James, Amy, Henry and Kathy who were quite grown up. Although he mourned his mother he was happy to be back; unknowingly, he was about to get the surprise of his life.

Henry was in his office when his secretary came in and said, "There is a mister Lee Breuer in the waiting room who says he is an attorney and would like to see you." After being shown in, a serious looking Mr. Breuer asked if Henry was Henry Phillips, the son of Bill and Eleanor Phillips, to which Henry said yes. Mr. Breuer then said to astonished Henry, "I am here to inform you that your real father is Mr. Henry Fielding and that he has named you as the sole heir of his sizeable estate." Mr. Breuer handed Henry a copy of Mr. Fielding's will and a testament signed by both Mr. Fielding and his mother Eleanor, stating that Henry is their son. Mr. Breuer then said, "I have DNA reports on your biologic mother and father, and if you give me a sample of your saliva, your lineage can be confirmed." The attorney then read off a list of Henry Fielding's assets, which included four large manufacturing companies, two banks, millions in securities and a vast portfolio of real estate. Henry was destined to become one of the richest men in Oregon.

Henry thought to himself that this explains a lot. He recalled watching with admiration imposing Henry Fielding as he intelligently lambasted the liberal city council, which explained where he got his intelligence and personality. It explained one of his lifelong questions, which was the reason he was so different than his mild, religious father Bill Phillips. It also explained why his mother had been so quiet over the years—she had had an affair with another man—and why the time he was leaving for New York she had grabbed him by the collar and said in earnest that his parents had loved him—apparently Bill knew Henry was not his son but raised and loved him anyhow, and his mother was afraid of losing Henry's love if he found out. Henry thanked the attorney and asked for Henry Fielding's address.

It was an emotional meeting. The next day Henry and John went to a mansion in a tony neighborhood of Portland, knocked on the door and told an expectant Henry Fielding they were his son and grandson. Henry Fielding was thrilled, told Henry he had followed his successful career with great interest and was impressed with his becoming a famous author. He took particular interest in John and asked him many questions about his life and work at Phillips Securities. It was a grand, fortuitous reunion of three generations of Fieldings that only got deeper when Henry Sr. met his grandchildren. Henry and John kept their last name Phillips, but in deference to their heritage, they changed the name of Phillips Securities to Phillips-Fielding Securities.

A few months later Henry was saddened when he learned that Tricia had died from a drug overdose. She had been a good friend who he thought had tragically succumbed to her own hyper authentic personality.

CHAPTER ELEVEN

Love and Chaos

After so much change Henry's life began to settle down. John, who had married and started a family, was promoted to president of Phillips-Fielding Securities, so Henry retired and was bumped up to board chairman emeritus. With his free time he started pursuing other interests, including his children, politics, his long-lost love Betsy and writing.

Henry was thrilled to get to know his children better even though most had left for college or graduate school. He was pleased to learn that they all had authentic personalities. Kathy, who was a senior in high school, was the only one left in the big house. She was a loving and friendly soul who worshiped her dad. James had the strong personality of his grandfather Henry Fielding, Henry III had taken after his father, Peter was bold and smart and Amy was confident like her mother Betsy—they all were in college. Peter, who was the most businesslike like his grandfather, father and uncle, was in graduate school in finance. It was Amy who saddened Henry because she reminded him so much of Betsy.

One unusual event during this period of Henry's life was seeing Ann for the last time. He got a call from an old high school friend asking if he was going to the thirtieth reunion. Now middle aged, Henry thought it might be fun, so he went and saw many longtime acquaintances. Henry was talking with someone when he felt this tap on his shoulder, turned around and saw a tired-looking, wizened old woman who he suddenly realized was Ann. They talked for a bit and then went outside to be alone. In spite of their rocky relationship and Ann's disloyalty, down deep they both felt a special kinship. They had been close childhood friends and knew each other intimately. They talked about their parents, their past together and their lives. Henry noticed that Ann was uncharacteristically pensive and thought to himself, like Tricia's authentic personality, her unauthentic personality had taken its toll. Her lack of self-respect and inner strength had diminished and beaten her. She had died inside. It was painful for Henry to hear her talk. She talked about her many disappointments, failures and problems in life. She told Henry she was poor, divorced and alone working as a waitress in a small café. Ann confided in Henry how her bad judgment had caused her to make many poor life decisions, the biggest one being losing him. She said her marriage to Ryan Peterson and fling with Clew Lewson were tremendous mistakes. They had been flakes, they had cheated and Ryan never supported their children. Ann smiled, looked at Henry for a long time, hugged him, said, "I wish I had married you," and with tears in her eyes, she said goodbye and left. Watching her leave, Henry recalled Oscar Wilde's comment that only the faithless truly know love's tragedies. He also thought that it could be the last time he would ever see her.

Things had not changed much in Portland while Henry had been away. There were still nightly riots in downtown Portland from anarchist fringe groups. Most storefronts had been boarded up, graffiti was everywhere, and there was extensive damage to public fixtures like fountains and lights and constant danger from mob violence. Because the police had been defunded, they were unable to stem the violence or even respond to urgent 9-1-1 calls. During the day downtown looked like a ghost town because most businesses had moved out and tourism and the convention business had dried up. It was also the same incompetent liberal Democratic leadership of Lew Day, Bill Huffy and Mayor Tim Weller. Weller was still unsure what to do, trying to satisfy everyone, still saying it's complicated and calling for another round of meetings. He was like Nero fiddling while Rome burned.

As an older and more experienced man, Henry decided it was time to confront the city council with the idea of making some changes in Portland's leadership. He picked one council meeting he knew would be televised, collected a few supporters like his dad Henry, son John and a few promising Republican politicians including Field Kasick. His timing was good because the citizens of Portland had grown disenchanted with the incompetent leadership and were open to change—for the first time the complacent Democratic leaders knew they could be facing the end of their careers. Henry started by saying how he had explained earlier to them why their liberal policies had failed and then launched into a powerful and convincing series of reasons why conservativism is a better political philosophy. At first Bill Huffy laughed out loud in a mocking way, which fired Henry's tongue.

First, he boomed, conservativism puts law and order first—civil society cannot exist in anarchy. This requires an ordered, reasoned and single-minded leader to enforce the law. His priorities should be to bring safety, protect property and punish the criminals. A new conservative leadership will immediately fund the police, call out the National Guard, establish a curfew, rigorously identify the criminal perpetrators and see that the district attorney prosecutes them. I guarantee the riots and violence will quickly stop! Huffy went conspicuously silent.

Second, conservativism will preserve citizens' freedom, which is a requirement for any good society. It eschews big, controlling totalitarian government that micromanages, directs and controls citizens' lives. It champions Emersonian individuality and self-reliance and militates against the progressive collectivism that makes citizens a small cog in a machine. It will bring greater individual freedom by offering consistency, allowing citizens to predict the future. Third, conservativism will preserve the best of the past, such as America's Founding Fathers' principles of life, liberty and the pursuit of happiness. Conservativism is unlike progressive policies and their oft repeated need for change that too often takes us further from those fundamental principles.

Fourth, conservativism is practical and works. It uses time-tested solutions like industry, effort and perseverance in order to make people's lives better. Fifth, it focuses on providing basic needs like shelter, food and medicine and keeps lofty and sometimes unrealistic ideals like perfect equality in perspective. To do this, it uses reason and relies on the scientific method to achieve results and not capricious compassion or sociology, which is the sixth reason. Seventh, and most importantly, conservativism champions capitalism because it brings prosperity and opportunity. Unlike socialism, it endeavors to build everyone up rather than pull some down, reward rather than incite envy and mirror and celebrate human nature rather than vilify and suppress it.

Eighth, conservativism's morality is grounded in reality with the social contract and not on shaky utilitarian stilts. Its ethics are timeless and more than the measure of man that demand personal responsibility and accountability. Under it there are truths that bring natural limits. Ninth, the individual and not government is the source of power and authority. Indeed, government is to remain unnoticed, constrained by low taxation, low debt and checks and balances. Finally, conservativism celebrates the human spirit. It liberates people and champions free will and individual potential—it is a political philosophy that builds self-worth and dignity.

Well, I am sure you are all now wondering why the god of love mentioned all this and what it has to do with love. In the beginning I told you that my story will involve some confusing things like politics and civil strife; the chaos and violence in Portland is an example. Love cannot thrive under uncivil circumstances, and Henry's loss of Betsy is just one example. The truth is love requires a future to exist because it entails anticipation and expectation. In civil strife there is only doubt and uncertainty, which denies future possibilities and the conditions love needs to exist. Unwittingly, Henry was taking the first steps to regain love. It turns out the listening public loved his lecture to the city council and voted in conservative Field Kasick and a majority of Republican council members, who quickly brought an end to the rioting. The police force was re-funded and strengthened and rioters were quickly apprehended and eventually prosecuted and fined or sent to jail. Portland then began a long period of recovery as downtown was restored, business gradually filtered back and citizens returned to the city sidewalks. Peace and predictability brought a new perspective to Henry and, surprisingly, a future with Betsy.

Just when Henry thought things were getting better, he read in the newspaper that Mark Finicus had been killed in an ambush by federal police officers. Henry recalled the fire-eater and how he had so passionately denounced urban liberal politics but was consumed by his own revolution. It was while Henry was pondering Finicus that Ellen Miller, Ann's mother, arrived and asked to talk with him in private. In a halting, emotional voice she told Henry that Ann had committed suicide a few days earlier. She paused and then said her daughter's last words were, "Please say goodbye to Henry for me and tell him I love him." She said Ann's life had steadily gone downhill since you split, that she had made poor decisions in life, especially about men, and eventually had turned to drugs for comfort. She said that Henry was the only man she truly loved in life and the one she forever regretted losing. Henry was devastated having lost his oldest friend knowing that as an unauthentic person who never experienced true love she had died long before her physical death.

CHAPTER TWELVE & CONCLUSION

Genuine Love

Ann's funeral was a small, rather depressing ceremony. It was held in an obscure church attended by only her mother, a daughter and a few friends. Neither her past husband Ryan Peterson nor any of her many boyfriends were there. The pastor, who did not know her, had little to say about her life other than how fully she lived it, which was not true. Henry just looked around feeling deeply saddened by Ann's awful and tragic life. The sad sight made him think of Betsy and how much he missed her.

Even though he felt lonely, he was optimistic because Oregon's politics had changed. It turns out there were many conservative like-minded people living in Oregon who had just let the leaders have their way but had become energized with Henry's televised speech. The old Oregon pioneer stock who traveled the Oregon Trail living in both rural and urban areas reasserted themselves and begin pushing the new interloper liberal Democrats out of the majority and reclaiming their heritage. They sent people like Bill Huffy packing. They had elected new conservative political leadership, including Field Kasick, the new mayor of Portland, and things quickly returned to normal.

It had been a long time since Betsy's arrest and trial but Henry decided to go over the details one more time. He went back and reviewed the police and court records, none of which had changed. Then he went to the news station whose video had been so conclusive in convicting Betsy. He studied the video of the riot and events over and over, taking special care to notice anything previously overlooked. There were many little things he recalled, like the scruffy looking motorcycle gang on the sidelines. He studied them in particular, and one mean-looking, hideously tattooed biker who seemed intent of egging everyone on. He noticed he gave one young person a bottle and another some cloth. He saw the club name on their jackets and tracked them down at their Unlucky Lady watering hole bar. They were a dangerous looking bunch of guys in leathers, but Henry was intent—when he saw the one from the video, he offered to buy him a beer and began to reminisce about the riot he had been in many years earlier where two federal police had been killed. The biker lit up and said, "Yeah. I killed them with a Molotov cocktail. It was so cool." Having second thoughts, he then told Henry that if he ever mentioned it to anyone, he would kill him. Henry went cold hearing this and left thinking he was glad to have recorded the biker, but he needed more evidence. Back in the news station Henry was going over the video again when he noticed a small strip of film at the bottom of the can. Excitedly, he played it, and to his astonishment it showed the biker throwing the cocktail at the police, catching them on fire.

With this new evidence, Henry rushed to the police, explained his situation, played them the recording and most damaging of all showed them the short video. The police acted quickly and sent the information to the district attorney, who presented it to a judge. The judge immediately ordered a new trial. Betsy was released, and the biker was arrested and charged with murder. Picking weak and tired but excited Betsy up at the federal penitentiary was one of the happiest events in Henry's life. They kissed and hugged and when they got home all their children, Betsy's family, Henry Sr. and John were there to greet her. It was a joyous reunion.

I was caught completely off-guard when Henry and Betsy reunited because I was unaware of a love higher than true love. I thought that true love occurs spontaneously, naturally and unconditionally between people who love themselves first and another for who they are. Betsy and Henry had reached this level of love earlier, which was a place of higher affection, a kind of timeless love irrespective of time and place. But I learned there is one level higher or more genuine, level-five love, which can only be reached by authentic people who risk their lives for one another. I saw it when Henry risked his life with the bikers to get the information he needed to free Betsy. Perhaps the movie *Tangled* demonstrated it best when Eugene cut off Rapunzel's golden hair thereby sacrificing his life for hers. It was a totally selfless act that cannot be explained rationally or philosophically—it is the essential characteristic of the highest form of love possible.

Having experienced this highest form of love, Henry decided to add a postscript to his book Authentic and Anonymous Character Types and Love, because he thought the book was incomplete without describing genuine love. He began describing love from the perspective of a person who had spent a good part of their life experiencing it. He wrote that many are content living solitary lives, but that is escapism. Certainly the workings of the heart can be strange and sometimes painful, but it is better to have loved, better to experience the pleasures of love and better to experience the human intimacy of love rather than the empty pursuit of desire. The right kind of love brings happiness because people connect on a primal emotional basis and they feel a companion in a lonely world that values them. And when in love they experience passionate affection, a sensuous world of delight, joy and happiness.

He wrote that his book had described four levels of love. The lowest are unauthentic and not true love. The lowest, or infatuation love, is just a one-sided feeling of awe, excitement and tenderness but is not other-regarding, and desire love is just self-gratification, mostly with sex, in which the other exists only for you. The upper two levels were authentic love. Love, or romantic love, is when you love yourself first and involves many things including kindness, devotion and respect for the beloved. Sex is a component but not the central bond. He then wrote he had thought the next level, or true love, was the highest form of love to be had, or the state when you love another for who they are. He wrote in his postscript that he had learned there was one higher love, or genuine love. Genuine love is when you lose love of self and become willing to die for another. It is a rare and timeless form of love that transcends the present in which your self-identity and your life merges with another and you become one.

Henry continued to write that few experience genuine love because it is so difficult to achieve, however experience had shown him there are certain ways of living that help. The first is to become the fourth kind of authentic person, which is the beginning of being able to control your desires and go beyond yourself and truly love. As Henry had learned from Betsy, it involves learning to be kind because it usually forgives and rarely punishes; you need to develop a personality that is virtuous that includes fidelity, loyalty and friendship; it helps to focus on the good in another and to minimize their negative traits; and you must also come to love yourself because it is the first step to lose yourself in another in genuine love

So, Henry finished his famous book and went on to live a happy and loving life with Betsy and his family. He did not write this in his book, but I think there is a kind of hierarchy within genuine love. Certainly, many kinds of people with different sexual proclivities can attain genuine love but, as I discussed earlier, the epitome is reserved for the man and woman who procreate children and nurture families. This relationship is utterly unique in that two beings that follow their natures create new beings from them in a crucible of love that endures throughout their lifetimes and perpetuates the human species. It is a simple formula consisting of a father, mother and children, and this is why Henry and Betsy were able to achieve the highest level of love.

ABOUT THE AUTHOR

John Bowman lives in Portland, Oregon, where he raised three daughters with his wife, Kathy. He is the author of numerous books on philosophy, real estate, politics, sports, words, Stoicism and humor. He received a Bachelor of Arts degree in 1973 from Whitman College, a Bachelor of Arts degree in philosophy in 1993 from Portland State University and a Master of Interdisciplinary Studies degree in philosophy and history in 2010 from Oregon State University. His master's thesis, titled *Stoicism, Enkrasia and Happiness*, surveyed the ancient philosophy of Stoicism and particularly the famous Roman Stoic Seneca. A complete list of his books follows.

The author welcomes reader comments, observations and rebuttals. His books and biography can be viewed on his website at www.johnlbowman.com, and he can be reached by email at author@johnlbowman.com.

Thanks for reading *Eros*, I hope you liked it.

Books by John L. Bowman

Reflections on Man and the Human Condition
Selected Topics in Philosophy
Nobody's Perfect
How to Succeed in Commercial Real Estate
Socialism in America
God's Lecture
A Reader's Companion
Stoicism, Enkrasia and Happiness
Aegean Summer
The Art of Volleyball Hitting
Graduate School
Provocative and Contemplative Quotations
On Law
A Reference Guide to Stoicism
A Reader's Companion II
Democracy and Why It Will Fail in America
Philosophy and Happiness
My Travels (unpublished)
How to Get Rich
A Reader's Companion III
On Humans
I Knew This Would Happen
Tupac
The Plague

9 780578 894669